Acclaim for J

"It isn't often that a writer of superlative skills knows enough about flying to write well about it; Saint-Exupéry was one; Salter is another."

—*The New York Times Book Review*

"He can bestow a powerful aura of glamour and heightened significance to even the most casual encounter. . . . His prose is . . . pure and ravishing."

—*The Nation*

"Sentence for sentence, Salter is the master."

—Richard Ford

"Nobody writes more beautifully." —Michael Herr

"[*The Hunters* is] a great American novel whose resurrection is long overdue." —*Forbes FYI*

"The pressure of Salter's high romantic soul animates his rich, crisp, neoclassical prose to bring us page after page of narrative magic." —Frank Conroy

"There is scarcely a writer alive who could not learn from [Salter's] passion and precision of language."

—Peter Matthiessen

JAMES SALTER

The Hunters

James Salter is the author of *A Sport and a Pastime, Light Years, Solo Faces, Burning the Days,* and *Dusk and Other Stories,* which won the PEN/Faulkner Award in 1988. He lives in Colorado and Long Island.

INTERNATIONAL

Also by JAMES SALTER

Burning the Days

Dusk and Other Stories

Solo Faces

Light Years

A Sport and a Pastime

The Arm of Flesh

The Hunters

JAMES SALTER

The Hunters

Vintage International
Vintage Books
A Division of Random House, Inc.
New York

FIRST VINTAGE INTERNATIONAL EDITION,
AUGUST 1999

 Published in the United States by Vintage Books, a division of Random House, Inc., New York, and simultaneously in Canada by Random House of Canada Limited, Toronto. Originally published in hardcover in the United States by Harper & Brothers, New York, in 1956. This edition, revised by the author, first published by Counterpoint, Washington, D.C., in 1997.

Library of Congress Cataloging-in-Publication Data
The hunters / James Salter. — 1st Vintage International ed.
p. cm.
ISBN 0-375-70392-6
1. Korean War, 1950–1963—Fiction. I. Title
PS3569.A4622H86 1999
813'.54—dc21 98-54900
CIP

www.vintagebooks.com

Printed in the United States of America
10 9 8 7 6 5 4 3 2 1

for W
who was my friend

PREFACE TO THE 1997 EDITION

The Korean War, in which the action of this novel takes place, was fought from 1950 to 1953. The geography of Korea and the sort of fighting that took place there were then familiar matters. Jet fighters were newly operational and the first combat between them occurred when pilots and planes from the Soviet Union were sent to support the communist armies of China and North Korea. They were opposed mainly by United States jets.

The Russian planes were swept-wing MIG-15s, well-designed and armed with rapid-firing cannon. There were many of them, flying out of airfields in China that for political reasons were never bombed. They were opposed by a smaller number of F-86s, a roughly equivalent aircraft, at the time the best in the U.S. Air Force.

The F-86 could not fly quite as high—to about 45,000 as against 48,000 feet—and its performance at high altitude was not as good, but lower down it was slightly superior. It carried machine guns with enough ammunition for—to give an idea of the brevity of the aerial engagements—only eleven seconds of firing, but a burst of two or three seconds in a fight could be quite sufficient. There were no missiles in those days; these came a few years later.

The basic combat formation was two planes and was called an

element: leader and wingman, meant to be inseparable. The wingman, usually a little less experienced, was a kind of bodyguard. His duties were nothing less than sacred: to serve as a lookout, especially when the leader was engaged with the enemy, and if needed, to support him with fire. Wingmen who had lost their leaders and vice versa were to immediately withdraw from the combat area.

A *flight* was made up of two elements and was the normal minimum force, although in a fight it often could not remain intact and broke into elements of two planes each. A squadron mission might involve three or four flights.

The chief defensive maneuver was a hard turn, the hardest possible, called a break, to keep another plane from getting into firing position behind. *"Break right!"* or *"Break left!"* was the urgent call when enemy fighters were closing in. Fighters don't fight, as Saint-Exupéry wrote, they murder, and the act was usually done by getting on the tail of the other plane, as close as possible, even point blank, and firing.

Aces are pilots who have downed five airplanes. They are champions. There were thirty-nine American aces during the Korean War. Their immortality was not as great as believed. At least one was himself shot down and killed. Others died afterward in crashes. Many of the aces were squadron, group, or even wing commanders, men often in the lead, aggressive and bold. Commanders were also shot down, at least five of them to my knowledge.

A small red star painted on the side of a pilot's plane, just below the cockpit, was the symbol of a kill. Discreet, almost invisible in the air, a row of five was a mark of highest honor, greater than any trophy or prize.

It was said of Lord Byron that he was more proud of his Norman ancestors who had accompanied William the Conqueror in the invasion of England than of having written famed works. The name de Burun, not yet Anglicized, was inscribed in the Domesday book. Looking back, I feel a pride akin to that in having flown and fought along the Yalu.

J. S.

The Hunters

1

A winter night, black and frozen, was moving over Japan, over the choppy waters to the east, over the rugged floating islands, all the cities and towns, the small houses, the bitter streets.

Cleve stood at the window, looking out. Dusk had arrived, and he felt a numb lethargy. Full animation had not yet returned to him. It seemed that everybody had gone somewhere while he had been asleep. The room was empty.

He leaned forward slightly and allowed the pane to touch the tip of his nose. It was cold, but benign. A circle of condensation formed quickly about the spot. He exhaled a few times through his mouth and made it larger. After a while he stepped back from the window. He hesitated, and then traced the letters C M C in the damp translucence.

It was a large dormitory room. There were ten double-deck beds and, as in all such places it seemed to him, no shelves, closets, hangers, or other furniture of any kind. The ceiling lights were protected by little wire cages, like those in a gymnasium. The building itself had evidently been a warehouse at one time. Its vast interior was filled with such rooms—the walls of bare concrete, the doors of riveted steel and set half a foot off the floor like those in a ship. He had come back from Tokyo a few hours before and, tired by a day of walking about and the seventeen-mile drive, had lain down for a few minutes before dinner. Sleep had taken him quickly. When he woke up, it was in the darkened room, alone. He felt beyond the inhabited world, isolated from all its life and activity. He stared through the steel-trussed panes of glass with weightless eyes, watching nothing. Night was coming quickly. The bare, thin trees were vanishing in the gloom, and lights were appearing in windows. He saw a pair of figures walking down the street side by side, not talking. They turned a corner and passed from his field of vision.

Cleve had spent four days in this replacement center, waiting for the orders that would send him on to Korea. All the time it had been among strangers, many of whom had just come from the war and were on their way, as lighthearted as children, back to the States. They passed him in loud, satisfied numbers. During his four nights, perhaps fifty different men had slept in the room, or at least dropped their bags there before heading for Tokyo. That was where most of them were now, he guessed. They left in the evenings and did not come back until the following day.

He picked up his towel and toilet articles and stepped across the corridor into the shower room. It was usually crowded in there, with a row of men standing before the steamy mirrors while water condensed in heavy drops on the ceiling and fell down upon them; but now it was empty except for a lean, towheaded man who could have been twenty-eight or thirty-eight, in the shower bin, singing away. His shoes, stuffed with socks, were on a bench just outside the bin—black, well-wrinkled flying boots. He stopped his song.

"Howdy," he greeted Cleve.

The spray was bouncing off the floor with a comfortable sound.

"How's the water," Cleve asked, "hot?"

"Hot as you'd want it. It feels pretty good on my old chilly bones, I'll tell you that."

"I'll bet it does."

"It'll soon put you right," the lean man explained amicably.

Cleve hung his towel on a hook and began to undress.

"What weather," he commented. "It's cold enough to wear your clothes in the shower."

"It's murder. Have you been to Korea yet?"

"No, I'm just going. How is it there?"

"I don't know. I'm on my way there myself. If it's like I think, though, we'll be missing this hot water."

"Among other things, I imagine."

Cleve stepped under the shower just as the lean man got out and began vigorously to dry himself. When he had finished, he slipped his bare feet into the boots, wrapped a towel about himself, and picked up his discarded clothes.

"See you," he said cheerily.

Cleve spent a long time allowing the warm flow to batter his shoulders and torso and make of his hair a thin, sodden cap. He felt both cleanliness and security, standing beneath the water, things that traveling deprived one of the soonest. Finally he turned the shower off, dried, and went back to the room to dress for dinner.

It was colder inside that vault than he remembered. He turned on the lights as he went in. Outside the windows it was full night, frozen and clear. Shivering a little, he took clean clothes from his bag and stuffed everything dirty into a compartment that was already almost full. Although he had been frugal with his laundry, he was close to running out. There was one clean shirt remaining, besides the one he had withdrawn to wear, and two changes of everything else. The only plentiful item was handkerchiefs. He put on his uniform, then his overcoat, and left the room, not bothering to turn out the light. He looked at his watch. It was almost seven, and he was very hungry. He strolled down the empty cement corridor, descended a flight of stairs, and walked out.

The night was illuminated by a bright moon that paled the stars, but despite this there was a thin haze, as if of frost, over everything. The buildings gleamed artificially through it. Every light was crowned with a delicate coronet. His footsteps splintered along the sidewalk, and his breath streamed in the air like silver evanescent smoke. This was a strange earth, Japan, and a brilliantly portentous heaven that covered it. He felt as if he were walking through a page of history. It was a disquieting sensation. He was moving in a current of destiny, quite alone, as alone as a man dying.

He had come a long way to this place. In the stale, crowded cabin of a transport he had sat for hour after hour while the night became day and the miles fell behind, unnoticed, so that it was like traveling through nothing but unbending time. From one horizon of the world to the other he had come, across endless waters, feeling continually more mortal and insignificant as he went, like a swimmer moving further and further from shore. Now he did not look back. The trip behind was a bridge gone. There was no returning. He had crossed to the war, and a great sense of excitement was on him.

Men often know what their destiny is to be, and perhaps Cleve knew his. If not, perhaps his eyes alone had seen it, for they were unusual eyes. They could be deeply, almost sadly, receptive, or as impervious as marbles. They were the most striking feature in a face that had composure, but of the mildest sort. Cleve wore no mask against the world. He had a mouth that smiled easily, a brittle nose, and a certain renown that seven years in fighters had given him.

It was a reputation based on achievement. One year, in the gunnery meet at Las Vegas, he had taken the individual air-to-air honors. He'd been on an acrobatic team, too, sweating doggedly through the monomania of formation loops and rolls too close to the ground. Afterward, there had been congratulations by generals and continued performances at the bar in the clubs, with more pilots than he could remember standing around listening to the talk. There was always a crowd, and singing and drinking. It was an exciting business, and nice to be pointed out.

It had gone quickly though, like the year of a first love, the delirious April suddenly a cool November. It had been a life like being at school, regulated and protected. There had been the moments of danger that could not be looked at too closely, and all the rest had been a swift passage of days. He was a natural flyer, not a cultivated one, and he had always known it: the ability had been there from the start; the amount of effort required to convert it into excellence had been small. It was like being a boy with a good memory in a history class. That was something you could be proud of, but never haughty.

He would sometimes recall, as if it had happened to another person, the compulsion to press close to death, to feel the purity that followed. He had always been respectful of the inner conquests of men and the rarefied, ascetic world they occurred in. He had traveled that world for a while, accomplishing he was not sure what, unless it was that he had learned a little of silence and perhaps devotion.

Friends on the outside were always asking why he stayed in, or telling him he was wasting himself. He had never been able to give an answer. With the fresh shirt on his shoulders still cold as ice, chilled from an hour in an unheated radar compartment at forty thousand feet between Long Beach and Albuquerque, the marks from the oxygen mask still on his face, and on his hands the microscopic grit of a thousand-mile journey, he had tried to find an answer sitting alone at dinner in the club filled with administrative majors and mothers talking about their children, but he never could. In his mind he carried Saturdays of flying, with the autumnal roar of crowds on the radio compass and the important stadiums thirty minutes apart and button-small, the wingmen like metallic arrows poised in the air above a continent, the last sunlight slanting through the ground haze, and cities of concrete moss; but never any reasonable reply. Or, sick of the stars and bored with speed on those nights in the great black sea, the surf of which was cities bubbling on the wave, listening to the others who were up, two unseen killers perhaps, calling themselves Butcher Red and seeking themselves in the darkness, he had tried to think of one—brief, understandable—but never could. It was all a secret life, lived alone.

One thing he was sure of: this was the end for him. He had known it before he came. He was thirty-one, not too old, certainly; but it would not be long. His eyes weren't good enough any more. With an athlete, the legs failed first. With a fighter pilot, it was the eyes. The hand was still steady and judgment good long after a man lost the ability to pick out aircraft at the extreme ranges. Other things could help to make up for it, and other eyes could help him look, but in the end it was too much of a handicap. He had reached the point, too, where a sense of lost time weighed on him. There was a constant counting of tomorrows he had once been so prodigal with. And he found himself thinking too much of unfortunate things. He was frequently conscious of not wanting to die. That was not the same as wanting to live. It was a black disease, a fixation that could ultimately corrode the soul.

He walked past some tennis courts with ice shining in patches on them and ivy like old string clinging to the fences, then came to the entrance of the club. It was warm inside. He looked about for a minute, feeling lost in the crowded room. Somebody against the far wall was beckoning to him. It was the lean man, eating dinner at one of the tables. Cleve sat down beside him.

"Have you eaten yet?" the lean man asked.

"No."

"It's a good meal tonight. Pork chops."

Cleve glanced at the menu and flipped it aside.

"Don't you like pork chops?"

"This waiting around is getting on my nerves."

"It can do that. I don't take you to be too high-strung, though."

"I'll be that way before long."

"How many days have you been here?"

"Four."

"I've been here three weeks," the lean man said. "Three weeks and three days, if you want to count it out."

"Three weeks?" Cleve was astonished. "My God, I hope you're an exception."

"There wasn't much I could do about it. I came down with some kind of virus just after I got here, caught it in San Francisco I expect, because I was sick enough on the trip across. They put me right in the hospital. I just got out a few days ago. I'm due to see the doctor again tomorrow morning; and if he thinks I'm all right, he'll clear me to get my orders to go on to Korea."

While Cleve ate, the lean man talked in his tart, unruffled manner, mostly about his experiences in the hospital. He had been given a fresh pair of pajamas every three days, he said, and after a while he began to develop a real interest in whether or not he would be able to complete his convalescence before he received any with a single button on them.

"How long are most people here?" Cleve asked.

"Oh, usually two or three days. Once in a while they're here longer. One fellow I heard of has been here over a month, but he's in Tokyo somewhere. They're still looking for him."

"He'd better hurry back or the war will be over."

"There's not much point in his hurrying now. He might as well take his time. He can't get in any worse trouble."

"I wouldn't think so."

"Some fool fighter pilot."

"Naturally, with that kind of independence."

The lean captain smiled.

"I guess I know what you fly," he said. "I was sort of hoping not. We might have ended up in the same outfit together."

"Not this war, I'm afraid," Cleve said.

"It was the same in the last one. You were in that, weren't you?"

"No."

"No? Well, wrong again. I'd have thought you were. A war is a war, anyway. I don't expect that there's much about them ever changes. I didn't really want to come to this one, but you know how it is. All the complaining. All the mothers and their innocent sons. It makes you go in spite of yourself."

The lean man went on talking. He seemed not so much soldier as wanderer, moving lightly through life with a sharp eye and a subdued sense of time. It was hard to tell about men like that, but Cleve could not help liking him.

They sat and smoked after the table was cleared and then, wordlessly agreeing, went into the bar. The crowd had preceded them. Slot machines rang with a continuous sound, and an uneven level of laughter and conversation supported some music being played at the far end of the floor where an orchestra was situated on a small stage. Japanese waitresses moved past in their neat uniforms, carrying trays of drinks. They were stocky girls, but graceful, with round scrubbed faces. A few were good-looking, and there was one who was exceptional, slender and well-formed. Her face had a rare calm quality. There was no way not to notice her.

"Not bad, is she, but she'd go hungry in Tokyo."

"What?" Cleve said.

"They have some mean competition there."

"I suppose so."

The orchestra was playing a medley of American musical comedy numbers. A few couples moved dutifully about the dance floor, as isolated as sails on a sea. The women were occidentals, all of them plain. One was buttoned in a prim blue uniform with a white patch of some sort on her shoulder and an overseas-type cap on her head. She appeared to be forty or more and was dancing with a solemn lieutenant. A third person could, with some difficulty, have passed between them.

There was a wave of cold air from the door being opened. Cleve looked up. A group of five officers had come in and were standing near the entrance, surveying the club. They were all second lieutenants, and it was obvious that they had arrived only recently, that night perhaps. The assurance was missing. They stood close together, relying upon each other. After a few moments they chose a table and sat down nearby. Cleve watched with no real interest as they discussed what they wanted to drink and summoned a waitress.

They were all identical, like the staff surrounding the emperor on a grand nineteenth-century canvas. There was just one who was misplaced. He was paler than the rest. He stood out like a strip of lemonwood in cedar and somehow seemed, comfortably, to be conscious of the distinction. The girl who came to serve them was the one Cleve had noticed. She stood obediently waiting. The pale lieutenant watched her coolly as he gave the order. She wrote it down and then slipped off. He whistled admiringly.

"How about that?" he said. "How would you like to get into that?"

"Who wouldn't?"

"I bet she'd do it for a pack of cigarettes, too."

"And you'd help her smoke them, eh, Doctor?

"Why not?"

Cleve heard the rest when she returned with the tray of drinks. He was not watching any longer, but there was the sound of the glasses being placed softly on the table.

"What's your name?"

"Myoko," quietly.

"Well, that's a new one anyway."

She did not answer.

"Don't you have another name, an American one?"

"No."

"How about Rita? That's a good name."

She was silent.

"How old are you?"

"Nineteen."

"Old enough, I'd say. What time do you finish work here, Rita?"

The lean man cleared his throat at this and turned toward the group.

"Say, friend," he said clearly, "lay off, why don't you?"

The lieutenant stared back through the dimness with bland eyes.

"What did you say?" he asked politely. The girl hurried away.

"I said that she'd lose her job if she went out with you. You wouldn't want that to happen to her, would you?"

"Are you the club officer or something?"

"No."

"I see. Just being helpful."

"That's right. She's not allowed to go out with any of the officers. It's a club rule. I thought you might not know about it."

"Thanks," the lieutenant said.

There was a brief, unnatural silence at the other table, and then Cleve could hear him talking again.

"How do you like that? If he was the club officer, I could understand it."

"Come on, Pell, we don't want to get in any trouble."

"Trouble? How's there going to be any trouble?"

"You'd better leave the girl alone."

"I'll talk to her if I want to. He's probably making a play for her himself. That's why he's bothered."

"You may get her in trouble, though."

"Wouldn't I love to?"

"I don't think you ought to fool around."

"Wait a while," Pell said. He settled back, apparently undisturbed, to sip at his drink and observe what was going on in the rest of the room.

Nothing more was said to the waitress by anyone at the table, however. The second lieutenants were loudly discussing flying when Cleve and the lean man left, quite a bit later. Through the cold night they walked back toward the barracks. The drinks after dinner had made Cleve sleepy. He listened to the sound of breathing as he undressed in his room, crawled into the deeply hollowed bedding of his iron cot, and was soon asleep.

Early the next morning, right after breakfast, he received his orders. They were what he had expected, assigning him to the most famed of the fighter wings, which was located close behind the front. It took him only minutes to pack his things. He was on the way at last. He did not catch sight of the lean man before departing.

2

It was almost noon when they crossed the Korean coast. Cleve stared anxiously at it, drifting past beneath the wing. He knew a moment of acute fulfillment, for here he would make a valedictory befitting his years. He had come a long way for it, and much was still ahead; but already he could feel self-imposed obligations, his burden of pride, diminishing, actually leaving him. He began to experience something of the exhilaration that came with triumph. In this war, he was more certain than ever, he would attain himself, as men do who venture past all that is known.

He looked about the cabin. Everyone was leaning toward the nearest window to see the land below, which lay calm as wreckage in the clear winter air. Not much could be distinguished to show where the war had been. Smooth fields of snow mottled everything, and the rivers were as pronounced as veins, but he did not think of an ancient mother of men. His eye was the flyer's. He saw the hostile mountains, the absence of good landmarks, and the few places flat enough to land in an emergency.

They had fought down there, on foot, taking weeks to move the distance he went in an hour. He was arriving like a tourist, in comfort. He felt the detachment of a specialist, and the importance. His gaze moved for a while to the heavy wing and the outboard nacelle, which was the only one he could see. A broad slick of oil, black and gleaming, was spread back from the cowling. He went back to staring moodily at the land.

Within an hour they had landed at Seoul. It was a blue, bitter February afternoon. Cleve stepped off the plane onto Korean ground frozen as hard as plaster. A sharp wind was keening across the flats. It stung his cheeks and made the rims of his ears ache. It came with the sharpness of steel into his lungs when he breathed. His eyes watered.

He followed along in the string of debarking passengers. They walked across a bare expanse of earth toward buildings near which were mounds of baggage, barracks bags, and groups of waiting men huddled in their overcoats. He walked past them and into the biggest hut. Inside it was crowded, too, and almost as cold. Men were clustered about the two oil stoves, warming their hands. Cleve hesitated, then began pushing through them with difficulty toward a counter he could see at the far end of the room. There he inquired, as soon as he had an opportunity to, about going on to Kimpo. He had no idea how long an additional trip it might be.

"I'll find out for you, Captain," the corporal said, turning away. "Hey, how do you get from here to Kimpo?"

"To where?"

"Kimpo."

"There's a bus that goes there."

"When does it run?"

"How should I know? Look at the schedule."

"Where's the schedule?"

"Oh, Christ." The other man walked over with an expression

of disgust on his face. He was a sergeant. He leafed through a foliage of paper tacked on the wall and quickly located the schedule. He ran a finger down its columns.

"The next one is due to leave here in," he looked at his watch, "thirty-five minutes." He turned to Cleve. "Are you the one who's going to Kimpo, Captain?"

"That's right."

"You can catch it just outside, on the road."

"Thanks."

Cleve sat down on one of the benches near the counter to begin an uncomfortable wait. He had meant to ask how long a ride it would be, but he suddenly felt it did not make any difference. He listened to pieces of conversation. Everybody seemed to be on the way back to Japan. In Japan, everybody had been going back to the States. He was moving alone against this tide. It was always that way, he reflected, the feeling of arriving late, after everything was over.

When half an hour had passed, he walked outside. There was no bus yet. He waited for five minutes, bundled against the wind. The warmth soon left him. A numbing cold penetrated the soles of his shoes and seemed to reach the bone. Finally, a truck appeared with a small wooden sign that said KIMPO wired to its radiator. He took his bags and threw them up over the tailgate. Then he went to sit in the cab with the driver. He was the only passenger.

They left the airfield, crossed a trestle bridge, and drove along the outskirts of Seoul. Everything seemed dirty and poor. The unfinished wood of the houses was blackened, and even the snow was gray on the roofs. It was a bleak, merciless time of the year.

Ragged children trailed begging after soldiers. The trees were bare, and outside the city the rice paddies were frozen. A few old men had chopped holes in the ice of the river to fish.

Cleve removed his gloves and lit a cigarette. There was not much taste to it, only a thin sensation of air that did not have the chill of crystal. He sat smoking as they jarred along. The road climbed and traveled an embankment overlooking an industrial section. Then it was lined with stunted trees for a way, before it emerged in open country.

"How far is it to Kimpo?" Cleve asked.

The driver shrugged. He had a plump, dull face framed in long sideburns.

"Fifteen miles, maybe," he said.

"Is the road this bad all the way?"

"It's about the same."

"Do you ever say 'sir'?"

The driver looked at him.

"Yes, sir," he said briefly.

The drive took three quarters of an hour. At the end they passed through a small, impoverished town, which was Kimpo. The airfield was just beyond it. The guard at the gate waved them through. Cleve had the driver take him to the wing headquarters. He got off there. It was a low brick building on the edge of the flying area. The nearest fighters were in sandbag revetments not fifty yards away, showing their clipped tails above the level of the bags, like dorsal fins.

Inside the headquarters it was reasonably warm. He unbuttoned his coat and took off his gloves, stuffing them into the pockets. A sergeant looked up from his typewriter.

"Can I help you, Captain?"

"I'm reporting in."

"Do you have copies of your orders?"

Cleve produced them. The sergeant read them hurriedly.

"You're Captain Connell?" he asked.

"That's right."

"Let me check with the adjutant," he said, leaving his desk.

He returned shortly. Cleve would have to wait for a few minutes, he explained. The adjutant was busy. Cleve nodded. He stood by the stove, idly, his thoughts a vague flurry of the journey that was now all behind him.

He became aware of a familiar sound in the background and turned quickly to the window to watch. A mission was taking off. He saw the first ships moving evenly across a visible length of the runway. Two at a time they went, leader and wingman, booming down the flat strip and then lifting easily up. The thin, dirty panes of glass before him rattled. Two more appeared, then two more, and two by two, in fierce majesty, trailing streams of black smoke, until Cleve felt impelled to try to count them. Colonel Imil was leading, north to the Yalu. A second squadron followed. Cleve watched until the final pair of ships faded in the distance, leaving silence behind them.

He knew Colonel Imil, the wing commander. He knew that monumental head and walk like a boxing champion. Dutch Imil, the grinning football player even after three teeth had been knocked out of his mouth one afternoon, the fourteen-victory ace of the second war, the first of the jet pilots, the golden boy, no longer really a boy, of the air force. Everybody who had seen him fly said that he was reckless, took too many chances, that sooner or later he was going to kill himself. He never did, though. He killed other men, but never himself. One rainy morning in Panama—Cleve had flown with him that day—he took sixteen ships up for a formation show over Balboa when the ceiling was only seven hundred feet. He lost two of them in the overcast, slung off against the mountains.

"The only thing a fighter pilot needs is confidence," Imil had said at the briefing, "and I've got enough for all of us."

Everybody had stories about him. They were as well known as old jokes. One Cleve had heard a long time before and never forgotten. Someone had told him that Imil had once been to bed with four different women in the same night. He was a brute, a big man. He was the kind of a man who could eat two steaks at a sitting, a man who found the normal world undersized in the shadow of his imposing body.

Cleve turned from the window and walked over to the stove again. He stood there, palming his hands to the heat. There was a strange mood here, he felt. He could not be sure what it was, an ill-fitting sobriety perhaps. He could see through an open door into the operations section. There was a large map of the peninsula stapled on the wall in there. It was covered, especially in the vicinity of the front, with military hieroglyphics of units and positions. The usual block of photographs was on the wall, too, in order of rank: General Muehlke, Far East Air Forces; General Breck, Fifth Air Force; then Imil; and lastly one he did not recognize, probably the group commander. Every office in the headquarters was decorated with that set, he guessed. For a few unreal minutes, a feeling that he had been in Korea much longer than two or three hours was generated in him. He remembered so many other headquarters, all alike.

"Cleve!" he heard someone shout.

He turned. A familiar face smiled at him, bright with cold.

Carl Abbott, wearing major's leaves. He seized Cleve's hand heartily.

"Hello, Carl. I didn't know you were over here."

"I haven't been long. Not as long as it seems, anyway. God, it's good to see you, Cleve. I heard you were on the way over. I've been on the lookout for you. Dutch has, too."

"How is he, the same as ever?"

"Exactly the same. He doesn't change. He's up on the mission right now."

"I saw it take off a few minutes ago."

"It's a routine sweep. He has blood in his eye today, though. Everybody has."

"What do you mean?"

"It's been a bad week," Abbott said in a strange, almost eager way. "I don't suppose you've heard, but yesterday we lost Tonneson."

Cleve listened to the story. Tonneson had thirteen MIGs to his credit, more than any other man. On the mission the previous day, he and his wingman had attacked a formation of twelve, and he had shot one down at the start, his thirteenth victory. As he slid into position behind another he was hit himself, solidly, just behind the cockpit. His wingman had stayed with him, orbiting, as he went down, calling to him to bail out, until the ship hit the ground and exploded. Abbott told it with an odd fluency, like a relish.

"It shook Dutch," he was talking faster. "I've known him a long time, and I can tell when he's nervous. He wasn't the only one either. Tonny was our top man. All the damned kids got the clanks when they heard about it. Well, you know how they are, anyway."

Cleve nodded. He knew how sensitive the common nervous system could be. He had felt it already, the subtle currents. Abbott, he noticed, seemed uneasy, unlike himself.

"We need you, Cleve. We need experience. Most of the old hands have gone, and we've been getting nothing but kids right out of flying school and gunnery. Eight of them came in last week. The week before that we got two men who had no jet time at all."

The flush from the fresh air had left his face, and a dull cast replaced it. There were heavy lines under his eyes. He looked old. Cleve could remember him as a young captain, five years before. They talked for a while longer, mostly about the enemy, what surprisingly good ships they flew and what a lousy war it was. The major repeated that despairingly several times.

"What do you mean, lousy?"

"Oh, I don't know," Abbott said distractedly, "it's just no good. I mean what are we fighting for, anyway? There's nothing for us to win. It's no good, Cleve. You'll see."

He trailed off uncomfortably, sorry he had started on this theme.

Abbott had been a hero once, in Europe in another war, but the years had worked an irreversible chemistry. He was heavier now, older, and somewhere along the way he had run out of compulsion. Everyone in the wing knew it. He aborted from too many missions. The airplanes he flew always developed some mechanical trouble, and he could be counted on to complete only the easiest flights. Colonel Imil had put him in group operations and was arranging a transfer to Fifth Air Force Headquarters. Everyone knew that, too.

It was part of the unashamed past for him to talk to Cleve,

who had known him only before, and he extended the conversation as long as he was able to. The others would get to Cleve soon enough. Finally, it was over. As Cleve left the building, he noticed for the first time that the flag was at half mast. He heard some ships go over, high, and looked up into the metallic sky for them. He could not see them, however. He found a ride going to the barracks area as the cold late afternoon came upon the field.

That night at the club everybody was there. Colonel Imil liked them all together. He knew that men could not think in such clamor, but only feel the warmth of shoulders against their own. It looked like a lumberjack camp. No two pilots were dressed alike. There were overcoats, leather jackets, woolen sweaters, and even a few plaid shirts. The room was a small one, filled with smoke and shouting. Beer cans and glasses were strewn on the tables. Imil was in the middle of it, and next to him Colonel Moncavage, the group commander. Moncavage was wearing a fur hat with the ear flaps tied together on top of it. He carried a .38 snubnose revolver in a shoulder holster, and a shining leather bandoleer studded with the brass butts of cartridges. Imil let out a bellow upon seeing Cleve. He waved him to his side and threw a great arm about his shoulders.

"Hey, Monk!" he shouted above the noise.

Moncavage turned.

"Come on over here. I want you to meet a real fighter pilot, Cleve Connell."

"How do you do?" the colonel said, shaking hands. He had been on a staff for some years before returning to command, and was still a figure of propriety.

"This is one of my old boys from Panama," Imil continued. "One of the best, too, eh, Cleaver?"

"Well, I . . ."

"I mean it, Monk," Imil confirmed, "one of the best."

Moncavage nodded, smiling wanly.

"Damned good to see you," Imil said. He pounded emphatically on Cleve's back. "I've been expecting you. Want to get yourself some MIGs, eh?"

"If they don't get me first."

"Still a comedian," Imil cried, grinning. "If they don't get you first. Listen, you bastard, I know you. You'll eat them up. You'll hit the glory road here, Cleaver, believe me."

Despite the mauling, a glow of pleasure rose in Cleve. It was good to be so cordially taken in. He let himself feel nothing but that.

"A gunnery champ, too, Monk, on top of it," Imil was saying. "Good eye and a fine pilot. We're damned lucky to get him."

"Did you just come in today?" Moncavage asked.

"Yes, sir. This afternoon."

"It's good to have you. What are you drinking?"

"Beer would be fine," Cleve said.

The colonel shouted toward the crowded bar, upon which at least twenty men were sitting, and three cans were quickly passed back to him.

"One thing we have here is plenty to drink," Imil grinned. "It's not much of a war otherwise, but what can we do? It's the only war we've got."

He treated everything with the kind of enthusiasm associated with sport. Cleve had never been able to feel very close to him, partly because of that. He was unable to share the attitude, which regarded life as only a continuing game. It seemed more impossible than ever just now.

Soon they were all standing on the tables, drinking and singing. Cans clattered to the floor. There were conflicts of shouting and laughter. Glasses were broken. Cleve noticed a few pilots he knew and spent some time circulating among them, exchanging greetings above the noise. All the others were strangers to him. Even the rosiest-faced of the youngsters looked like veterans, though, in layers of heavy clothing, with pistols hung from their hips or under their arms. He overheard two of them talking about some major. He had been an ace in the last war and an instructor in the training command afterward. He had over three thousand hours and *takusan* jet time.

"But, you know," one of them said, "he's not too good at, well, at judging the space-time relationship in the air. Do you know what I mean?"

"Not exactly."

"What I'm trying to say is that he can't fly."

"He won't fight, either. I don't know which is worse."

"The son of a bitch. And I get scheduled with him almost every time he goes on a mission."

"He won't be around much longer."

"I don't know. He'll never get shot down, though; I'm sure of that."

Imil was slowly doubling an empty can with one hand, not paying much attention to it as he did.

"He's a little different," he told Moncavage, "maybe not always ready to tell you how good he is, but take it from me. After a few weeks, when he gets a taste of things, you'll see."

"He looks competent enough, I'll say that."

Imil laughed. He tossed the folded can to the floor.

"Don't strain yourself," he said.

"It's an observation, that's all."

"My bet is he has a MIG before you do."

"I don't know about that," Moncavage answered quickly.

Imil glanced down at him, a head shorter and lightly built.

"That bothers you, eh?"

"I've been away from flying for a while," Moncavage began, "I don't deny it. . . ."

"What are you trying to say?"

"If it's something you'd like to bet on . . ."

Imil slapped his shoulder jovially.

"You're coming along. I wanted to see what you'd say."

"Don't worry about me."

"You'll be all right. Just make sure you keep a good wingman with you, that's all," Imil grinned.

Moncavage was silent. He'd only had the group for a short time. He knew he wasn't trusted yet and was working to overcome that. Vaguely he'd begun to fear that he never would. Imil commanded the wing in a heavy-handed way. He never hesitated to intercede in group matters. Moncavage resented that. It was going to be a long, defensive struggle for him to come into real command. He knew he wasn't stronger than Imil, but he felt he was smarter.

"Make sure he's a flight commander pretty quick," Imil said. "He can work on up from there."

Moncavage said nothing. You run the wing, and I'll run the group, he thought to himself. He'd rehearsed the phrase before. He nodded in agreement though. He wished he had started calling Imil, a fellow colonel not three years older, Dutch, from the beginning. That, he realized, would have made things better. It was too late now. Self-consciousness had set in. He was even feeling uncomfortable about his trim, soldierly appearance as contrasted with Imil's, which, while not sloppy, was tough and bearish. He watched as Imil took a last drink of beer and began to crush another can.

As it grew late, the party seemed to intensify. It was going stronger, with the room more crowded, if that was possible, than it had been earlier. Cleve finally left about midnight.

Outside, it had started to snow. Through the darkness swirled a white mist of flakes too delicate to stick to anything. They brushed against his face and made the air seem fresher to breathe. As he walked along the road back to his room, he could hear the subdued sound of singing all the way. When the door slammed behind him, though, the sudden quiet was overwhelming. He sat down on his cot and untied his shoes. He was tired. Somehow, he had the feeling of Christmas away from home, stranded in a cheap hotel, while the snow fell silently through the night, making the streets wet and the railroad tracks gleam.

3

He was assigned to a squadron. He had to go through a brief training program that involved three or four flights behind the lines, mostly to practice the formations and tactics employed by the group. There were also some lectures on combat procedures, use of the radio, navigation aids, recognition, codes, and so forth. It was all very informal, and the biggest thing was to accomplish the preliminary flying. Aircraft were available only between missions, which usually meant in the middle of the morning or afternoon. Frequently there were none to spare, so for a number of days he had little to do. In bed in the mornings, he could see the sky through a window, a rectangle of blue between the tiled roofs of the buildings.

On the fourth morning, he woke up early. The sky, he noticed, was topped with a high layer of cirrus, as even and regular as the roof tiles or a cobbled street. For a while he lay still in the warm bedding. He could hear the first-light reconnaissance ships running up their engines at the near end of the strip. Beneath the eaves of the barracks the sparrows scurried, ruffled by the wind, giving chilled cries.

It was an effort to swing his feet out over the cold concrete floor and put on his shoes. He did it finally in one hurried moment, not without shivering. Up at last, he shaved in a pan of water that had been on top of the stove all night. It was as hot as a man could stand. He rinsed the shaving cream off with clear hot water dipped with a canteen cup from another container that had been on the stove, and then opened the door and threw it all from the pan onto the bare, hard earth outside. It steamed as it hit the ground and sank in. Then he combed his hair before a blackened mirror, put on a woolen shirt, sweater, and flying jacket, and stepped out to walk down the road to breakfast. The cold air made his nose run and shocked his eyes into complete awakeness.

The Korean mess boys brought him his food on a tray: salty bacon, eggs, toast, and steaming coffee poured from steel pitchers. When he had finished, he smoked a cigarette. This was, so early, contrary to a mild resolution of his, but he did not resist the desire. He made of it the first of that day's concessions to the shortness of life. After a while he got up and started walking down toward the flight line about a mile away. It was a cold, damp morning. There was a raw wind that made his bones feel brittle. The sun was just rising, its light low across the hills and over the flatlands in which the field was located.

The first mission was taxiing out. The ships, some painted with black-and-white zebra stripes, others with a solid band of yellow, moved along quickly, but they seemed strangely inept on the ground, rolling like cable cars or trolleys. A few of them had red stars stenciled under the cockpit rim. He saw the pilots hunched inside, faceless and inhuman under the helmets and black oxygen masks.

They lined up in pairs on the runway, twelve ships altogether. The engines were run up. The smoke shot backward and skyward. A sustained roar filled the air, a deafening eruption, like an ultimate wind of flame. The noise was brutal, but deep and assuring. It seemed endless. The rear ships quivered in the river of blast. He watched the first two finally go, their rudders flicking slowly from side to side as they began to roll, like the tails of fish holding quietly against a current, rolling very slowly at the start and then quickening until they flowed down the far end of the runway and nosed into the sky. The others followed at close interval.

Desmond was the squadron operations officer, and Cleve had known him, too, in Panama. He was in his office listening to the command radio when Cleve walked in. The whole mission could be followed like that. It was the way the broadcast of a football game would be if there were a microphone in the huddles.

"Sit down, Cleve," he said. He motioned toward the radio. "They're just going out."

"I saw them on my way down here."

"I don't expect there's much of a chance of their running into anything. It's too early. The MIGs haven't been flying this early."

"I'd like to listen, though."

"Oh, I'm not going to turn it off."

Cleve stood by the stove to warm himself. A number of the other pilots wandered into the office individually, but none of them stayed long. Desmond introduced Cleve to them when they came in. The encounters were reserved. Cleve felt the calm suspicion with which they regarded him, a newcomer. After a few quiet words, they would ask if there was anything happening on the mission. Then they would leave. There was little coming in over the radio. The ships were still heading north. It was two hundred miles to the Yalu.

"How are the training missions coming along?" Desmond asked.

"Oh, splendidly. The only question is, are there enough of them?"

"Everybody has to go through the same thing, Cleve."

"I know, I know. Will I be able to fly today?"

"If we have ships to spare, you will."

"I feel like I've been here a month already."

The radio interrupted. It was nothing, however, except a few laconic comments.

"It's still too early," Desmond decided, looking at his watch. "Usually, if there is a fight, it starts right on the river."

"Don't the MIGs ever come south any distance?"

"Not very often."

"Why is that?"

"They don't have to, unless they're out to get the fighter-bombers, say. They know we'll come to them wherever they are. It's even to their advantage. We have to fly two hundred miles up there to fight and then two hundred miles back, but they're always within sight of their own fields."

Cleve nodded. There was a pause. Running his thumb along the edge of the desk, as if testing its sharpness, he said, "How good are their pilots?"

"It depends which you're talking about, the good ones or the bad ones."

Cleve did not interrupt.

"When they're good," Desmond said, "they're damned good; but there aren't too many of those. The rest are pitiful, worse than students sometimes. I've seen them bail out just because they were scared. The only trouble is, well, take Tonneson, for instance. He didn't think much of them. He used to say there were none of them worth a damn. They couldn't fly, and they couldn't shoot. He was convinced of that, and then he ran into some that could. The trouble is, you never know what you're up against, so you can't afford to make mistakes. On the other hand, there're some guys like Abbott."

"What about Carl?"

"He doesn't know there's a difference. He's afraid of them all."

"He shot down six Germans."

"That was years ago. I'm telling you the truth. Everybody knows it. He just hasn't got it anymore."

"I can't believe that."

"You will," Desmond assured him. He laughed bitterly. "He's the only man I've ever seen who could abort from a mission and then write up the airplane as OK when he landed. I'm not exaggerating a bit, either. It's a sad case. There are good MIG pilots, but after all . . ."

"What are the good ones like?"

"They're tough. If they get behind you, you don't shake them off with one hard turn. They'll stay with you, all the way down to the deck a lot of times. It's happened to me. About all you can do then is hope they fire out or run low on fuel, or that somebody shows up to help you. If it's really one of their *honchos* back there, you're just out of luck. All you can do is turn as hard as you can and keep hoping."

"That's what makes it a war, I suppose," Cleve said. "You shoot at them, they shoot at you."

"That's right. What could be fairer?"

"Nothing."

"The only thing is to play it smart. You never know who you're running into. It's probably some cull, but it might be old Casey himself."

"It might be who?"

"Casey Jones."

"Who's that?"

"Do you mean it?" Desmond said. "I thought he was pretty well known."

"Not to me. Who is he, the great Russian champion?"

"I don't know. He flew a black-striped ship, very distinctive. Ask Imil about him sometime. He can tell you. Only don't believe everything he says.

"He came back with three cannon hits on his ship one day. He was lucky to even get back. There was one right in front of the cockpit that left a hole you could stick your head through, and two more just as big in the wing. That was Casey. According to the story, they fought for about twenty minutes, and the colonel didn't even get a chance to fire his guns. He looked like he'd had a heart attack when he landed, I know that much. I saw him at the debriefing.

"When I first got here, every time Casey flew, there was a big fight. They used to know when he was taking off, I don't know how, but ground control would call him off by name. The MIG formations were trains, so they called him Casey Jones. Train number one, or whatever it was, leaving Antung, Casey Jones at the throttle. When you heard that, you started watching yourself, too."

"What became of him?"

"I guess he finished his tour and went home. He just stopped flying. It's been a long time since anybody's seen him."

They listened to the mission then, but Cleve sat preoccupied, with thoughts of a vanished enemy. He had gone, this man whose name no one knew, taking his excellence with him. The skies were empty now of the fever of his presence; and Cleve, though he had not fought, resisted a feeling of personal loss. Something irreplaceable had been taken from the war. He felt cheated. It was only after some time that he was able to suppress the whole thing as illusion. It was always the old ones who were the greatest.

Nothing much seemed to be going on, up north. There were long periods of silence, broken only by turns being called and fuel checks. Finally, they began heading back, no sightings. Desmond turned the radio off.

"How often do you get into fights?" Cleve asked.

"You can't ever tell when there'll be one. Sometimes there are three a day, and sometimes a week will go by without one. It's like trying to pick the horses. You check everything, the past performances, who's up that day, the weather, the odds. You get it all doped out, and then it's luck after that. How's your luck, Cleve?"

"It's been pretty good. Nothing exceptional."

"That's all you need. I'll take a lucky man every time, myself."

There was a pause. Desmond sat looking out the window toward the mountains that rose in the north. The ships would be returning over them in fifteen or twenty minutes.

"If you really want to get them, Cleve," he said at last, "more than anything else, that's the biggest thing. You can play it safe and never get in a tight spot, and you'll go home after a hundred missions with the usual medals and, who knows, maybe a couple of victories, just by waiting for the sure things. On the other

hand, you can take chances, and you'll probably be a hero when you go back. And you'll probably go back. It just depends on what you want most. You'll see for yourself. After ten missions everybody is an expert.

"Victories mean a lot, but as far as I'm concerned, there's something more important to be gotten out of Korea."

"What's that?"

"My ass."

Cleve laughed.

"That's the way I feel," Desmond said.

For a naked moment, they looked at each other. It had been a genuine confidence, and Cleve knew then how good his chances really were. Whatever the advantages of ability, there was something even more important. It was motive. He had come to meet his enemy, without reservation. The discomfort was there, even after talking to Desmond, of perhaps encountering one that would prove his equal; it was always a chance, but, even so, he felt encouraged. He had not come merely to survive. He suddenly felt the uplift of being that much above those who had, who lived on a subordinate plane of endeavor.

4

At 5:15 in the morning it was piercingly cold, with an icy moon still bright in the sky. The windows of the barracks were dark as Cleve walked down the road to where a truck waited in front of the mess, its parking lights on and an asthmatic smoke wreathing from its exhaust. The mud beneath his feet was frozen into hard ridges and swirls. The cold bit at the tips of his fingers through his gloves. He had given up eating breakfast on mornings like these. The result was an insistent hunger later on, but he preferred the extra sleep. He had finished all the training flights and indoctrination. During the week past he had started flying missions. There had been four of them, all uneventful. This was to be his fifth. He was scheduled on Desmond's wing.

After the briefing, they dressed in a locker room grim with the light from the early day and a single unfrosted bulb. Desmond always loaded himself with equipment in excess of that which everybody carried in standard seat packs. His pistol he wore at his waist, the holster tied down against his thigh with leather thongs. On the other hip was a heavy hunting knife and a canvas packet of extra ammunition clips. Besides that, he filled his flying-suit pockets with plastic boxes of jellied candy, cigarettes, and hand warmers, wrapping friction tape on the outside of the pockets to hold them firmly. Everything had to be secured or it would be lost upon bailing out, ripping right through cloth at the shock of the parachute opening.

There was some erratic humor. Robey, one of the flight leaders, read an imaginary telegram he had received from Big Stan Stalenkowicz—"You all remember him as tackle on last year's team." Stan was going to be at the game today, and he wanted they should get out there and really fight. In reply, there were some pledges to win this one for Big Stan.

Robey was credited with four victories. He was the leading man in the squadron, and he did not look the part at all. He had a small, pale mustache, which seemed to have been pasted as an afterthought onto the face as bland as a piece of fruit. His complexion was bad. The one thing that distinguished him was the self-assurance of an heir. One more aircraft destroyed, and he would have his title. Because of this, he was treated with deference. In return, he was patronizing. He moved among them as if they were, even unknowingly, his flock.

"Going to open up a hardware store, Des?"

"Very funny."

Cleve dressed himself slowly to reduce the time he would have to spend standing around and taking little part in the talk. He was not fully at ease. It was still like being a guest at a family reunion, with all the unfamiliar references. He felt relieved when finally they rode out to their ships.

Then it was intoxicating. The smooth takeoff, and the free feeling of having the world drop away. Soon after leaving the ground, they were crossing patches of stratus that lay in the valleys as heavy and white as glaciers. North for the fifth time. It was still all adventure, as exciting as love, as frightening. Cleve rejoiced in it.

They climbed higher and higher, along the coast. It became difficult to distinguish earth from water where they met. The frozen river mouths blended into white land areas. The rice paddies south of Pyongyang looked like cracked icing on pale French pastry. He saw the knotted string of smoke go back as Desmond test-fired his guns. He checked his own. The sound of them was reassuring.

They climbed into the contrail level. Long, solid wakes of white began flowing behind them. Formations left multiple ribbons of this, streaming sky pennants. Frost formed on the rear of Cleve's canopy. He was chilly, but not uncomfortable. They were north, and he was busy, looking hard, clearing himself, Desmond, and the two other ships in his flight. The sky seemed calm but hostile, like an empty arena. There was little talking.

In half an hour they had reached the Yalu, an unreal boundary winding far below. The sun was higher now. The sky was absolutely clear. His sunglasses made it a deeper blue, like deep ocean. He could see a hundred miles into a China that ended only with a vast horizon, beyond the lives of ten million rooted people. At forty thousand feet they patrolled north and south, turning each time in great, shallow sweeps.

They had been doing this for about ten minutes when somebody called out contrails north of the river. Cleve looked. He could not see them. Then he heard,

"They're MIGs."

He heard Desmond: "All right, drop them."

He dropped his tanks. They tumbled away. He looked north. Still he saw nothing. He was leaning forward in his seat, intently. He stared across the sky with care, inch by inch.

"How many of them are there?" somebody asked.

"They're MIGs!"

"How many?"

"Many, many."

He looked frantically. He knew they must be there. He began to suffer moments of complete unreality. He felt he was staring holes in the sky.

"Where are they crossing?" somebody called.

"Just east of Antung."

Then at last he saw them, more than he could count. It seemed unbelievable that he had been unable to locate them only seconds before. He could not make out the airplanes, but the contrails were nosing south unevenly, like a great school of fish. They were coming across the river. They were going to fight.

Soon they were near enough to distinguish: flight after flight of from four to six ships, the flights in a long, tenuous stream, all above them, at forty-five thousand, he guessed. The van of this column was approaching fast. Suddenly, he understood why these formations were called trains. He expected the fight of his life momentarily.

"Let's take it around to the right," he heard Desmond say.

They started a turn toward a position beneath the MIGs, with unbelievable lassitude it seemed, and began traveling south with them. Cleve felt very alone in the cockpit. He was acutely aware then of being far into enemy territory. He squirmed in his seat. His mouth and throat were dry. It burned to inhale. Still they went south, the MIGs staying above. It was like watching a fuse burn.

At that altitude they could not climb the five thousand feet up to the MIGs without losing speed and falling behind or else leaving themselves almost motionless in the air to be attacked, so they continued underneath and a little to one side, watching the ships and contrails floating high above like the surface after a deep dive. Cleve was shocked by the number of them. He could count more than fifty. At that moment he had only one friendly flight besides his own in sight. There were sixteen friendly ships altogether, four flights.

Suddenly, the radio exploded with voices. The fight had started somewhere. He felt his nerves twitching. Then there were four of them, Desmond called them out, turning down for a pass. They did not come all the way, however. They swept overhead, going at an angle. Cleve saw them closely for the first time. He watched the nearest one sail across, silver and abrupt, with speed fences on the wings, as soundless as a great fish. Then they were gone.

Two others started down in a high side pass. They turned into them, and the MIGs pulled up and continued on. It was all sparring. Desmond was cautious. He kept them out of trouble, but constantly turning so that there was little chance for him to make a pass himself. He flew like a boxer who keeps moving away, waiting for an opening.

Even though Cleve could see the MIGs easily now with the contrails marking them plainly at great distances, he still had a pressing sensation that they might be coming in from all sides, unseen. He sweated, twisting in the cockpit, straining to look everywhere. They turned indecisively among the MIGs for about ten minutes. Once he saw one firing at him from a long way off. The cannon shot firm, heavy tracers that arced through the air like Roman candles.

Finally, he and Desmond were chasing four of them north, unable to close; and when they broke off, it was all over. The MIGs were gone, vanished, as characteristically as they had appeared. The sky was empty except for the fading traces of contrails, left like ski tracks in blowing snow.

They turned toward home. Cleve felt tired. As he listened to the talk of the withdrawal over the radio on the way back, he realized that he could not remember having heard anybody except Desmond after they were once in it, he had been so absorbed.

"It looks like they came up early in the morning for a change," Desmond said when they had landed and were waiting for the truck to throw their equipment on and ride back to operations, "but it wasn't much of a fight."

"No, it wasn't," Cleve agreed, although he felt very spent.

"They were too cagey today. It's usually like that when the fight is in the cons. They can see you too easily, and you can't get close to them. Not only that, but they just didn't seem to want to mix it up this time."

"I thought they were doing their share."

"What do you mean?"

"It seemed we were playing it pretty safe," Cleve said.

"You got back, didn't you?" Desmond said flatly.

"So did they."

There was a silence. Cleve regretted having said it.

"You did a good job, Cleve," Desmond said simply.

"Thanks." He thought with despair that it had not been as he had anticipated, easy fight or not. He was going to have to push himself beyond what he had expected. A sense of inadequacy made him feel exhausted and as fragile as a dry stalk.

At debriefing they learned that Robey had gotten his fifth. It was the only kill claimed. He was standing in a crowded circle at one of the tables, grinning and being congratulated, telling the colonels how he had done it. Imil was beaming, and even Moncavage nodded his head happily. Cleve followed Desmond into the group to shake the triumphant hand.

"How did you get him, Robe?" Desmond asked.

"On a head-on pass. I got some good hits, and he bailed out. At forty thousand. Opened his chute at forty thousand, too. He's probably still floating down."

"Nice going."

"Thanks."

"Congratulations," Cleve said.

"Thank you."

They moved aside. Other men were pushing in to hear about it. As they walked away from the building, somebody asked Desmond what had happened.

"They were up."

"How many?"

"Seventy or eighty, I guess."

"Did anybody do any good?"

"Robey got one."

"A kill?"

"Yes."

"That unconscious bastard. Nobody else?"

"Not that I know of."

"Did he really get this one for a change?"

Desmond did not answer. They walked on. It was still early in the morning, just after eight. If they drove to the mess, they might be able to get something to eat, even though it was after breakfast hours. When they were driving along a few minutes later, Cleve asked about the remark.

"I won't say he didn't get them," Desmond replied, "but two of them were pretty doubtful."

"How does he get credit for them if there's any question?"

"All he has to have is his wingman's confirmation, whether his film turns out or not. First, it's a damage; he thinks he saw a couple of hits when he was firing. Then, when he talks to his wingman after they land, they decide it must have been a probable; and at debriefing they get carried away listening to the other claims, and it's turned into a kill."

"How often does that happen?"

"It happens. Robey's first one, for instance. He was up around Sinanju with his flight, going north, and they made a head-on pass with some MIGs at about thirty thousand. That was all there was to it. By the time they were able to turn around, the MIGs were gone. When they got back after the mission, Robey claimed the one he was shooting at. Dawes was his wingman, but he wouldn't confirm it. He said he hadn't seen a thing. All he'd admit was that they saw a column of smoke on the ground a little later. Robey said that was where the MIG had crashed.

"Well, it was at a time when there hadn't been any action for about a week or more, and Dutch was particularly anxious to see kills; so he took Dawes aside and talked to him. You can imagine what that was like. Dawes was a second lieutenant.

" 'Now, Dawes,' he said, 'you understand that Captain Robey can't get credit for that MIG he shot down unless you confirm it, don't you?'

" 'Yes, sir,' Dawes said.

" 'All right. Then you did see him do it, didn't you?'

" 'No, sir. That's just it. I didn't see a thing. I was shooting, too.'

"'Try to remember, Dawes,' Imil said. 'It may have all happened quickly, but you did see that MIG go down, didn't you? Think back. Think hard.'

"'No, sir. I really didn't.'

"'You're not trying to remember, Dawes. Think. Think of your career, Dawes.'

"'As a matter of fact,' Dawes said, 'I do seem to recall seeing that MIG smoking.'

"'Certainly you did.'

"'Yes. That's right. It was on fire. Now that I think back, I remember it. He got it, all right. There's no doubt about it.'"

"Is that the truth?" Cleve said. He was not easily shocked.

"Ask Dawes."

They sat down to coffee and toast. Several people stopped at the table to ask about the mission. News of it had traveled with incredible speed, Cleve found. He still felt no more than a meager satisfaction at having participated in it; but he was also aware of some sort of mystic fulfillment, as if the fight were a kind of nourishment or a violent poison, repeated small doses of which would eventually confer immunity.

5

Cleve was made a flight commander a few days later. The four flights in the squadron lived in a single long barracks in which each had its own room. After the houseboy had moved his bag in and made up a cot, Cleve came in himself.

It was a large room, but crowded, with walls of a sooty white. There was a debris of furniture that had been made from the wood of packing crates: wardrobes, cabinets, a ponderous table, and several awkward chairs. A mosaic of women in clippings of every size was on one wall from the ceiling down almost to the floor, and four or five feet wide. Cleve was overwhelmed by the litter. The windows had occasional squares of cardboard for missing panes, and not much light came through them. Near the door was a long wooden rack loaded with good uniforms for leave in Japan, steel helmets, overcoats, and gas masks. It made entering the room like coming into a den.

Four men were sitting around the center table, talking, when he came in. Two of them, the second lieutenants, had moved in only a few days earlier. An air of idleness surrounded them all. They had endless time before them, it seemed, in this waiting room of some isolated station. Whatever conversation they had been having was suspended as they greeted Cleve. He had met them all previously; but as he unpacked and began talking to them for what was really the first time, he felt the mutual sizing up, as if they were being cast adrift in a small boat together.

DeLeo, who had lived there next to the longest, stood up and went to a window, slid it open, and reached out into a wooden box nailed facing the casement.

"A beer?" he asked Cleve. "They're ice cold."

"So am I; but thanks, I'll have one."

DeLeo extracted three cans. He carried them back to the table and opened them. He handed the first one to Cleve and the second to Daughters. Then he sat down and picked up his own. He was tall and capable looking, with black hair and an exaggerated black mustache. His teeth were very white and even.

"Well, here's good luck to you, Captain," he said, "from your new boys, such as they are. You're not getting much to work with, I can tell you that: an arithmetic teacher, a wop, and two eagle scouts."

"All right. I'll drink to that. You're not getting so much either."

"That's not what I hear."

Cleve felt the glances of the lieutenants on him as he drank. They were looking toward him casually, but with respect.

"Before it passes unchallenged," Daughters said, "I wasn't an arithmetic teacher. He just likes the sound of that. I actually coached the baseball and basketball teams and only filled in as a teacher."

"What do you want me to call you?" DeLeo said. "Coach?"

"Sure. That's all right."

"One of the hardest things in life is to separate the details from the important points. In this case, the coach part is incidental.

History will remember you as an arithmetic teacher and ignore the incidentals."

"That's very interesting," Cleve said. "You're not by any chance a history teacher, are you?"

"Me? A teacher?"

"Why not?"

"I'm a wop," DeLeo said, smiling broadly, "that's all; but let's face it, incidentally there's a little bagel in me, too."

DeLeo came from a tough mining town in West Virginia. He was one of those men who seem to have arisen from a place spontaneously, with neither family nor enduring friends having marked his growth. He would shrug when asked what he had done before being in the service. It was authentic. He seemed to be completely independent of obligations.

Daughters was different, a man enmeshed in the complexities of life, thin and preoccupied. He was about the same age as DeLeo: they were both in their late twenties. Daughters had flown during the last war, but his only overseas service had been in Iceland, and he had not seen any combat. He had been discharged and had coached and taught in a high school in New Mexico. He had a wife and three small sons there. As a reserve officer, he had been recalled to the service in 1950, and he was fulfilling his duties without complaint, but also without any soaring enthusiasm. He wrote long, regular letters home. He had flown thirty-one missions when Cleve took over the flight. DeLeo had twenty. The two second lieutenants had not flown any.

"There's your real problem," DeLeo said, waving his hand toward them casually, "the air cadets."

"Aw," Billy Lee Hunter protested.

He was tall and husky, a Texas boy shining with artlessness. He was just out of gunnery school. In his home town the proud parents read his letters to all the neighbors and other folk around.

"I don't mind being kidded," Hunter went on, "but I surely am anxious to start flying missions."

"The same for me, too, sir," Pettibone added. He was the other second lieutenant. His cheeks looked as if they had been slapped into rosiness, and his fine hair was like a cap of gold.

Both of them had been sitting quietly side by side since Cleve had come in, like two spinsters at a cocktail party, listening to the conversation but saying nothing, a partially empty beer can in front of each. Now they eagerly took the opportunity to talk.

"They surely do ride us a lot," Hunter explained innocently, "but I suppose they had to take it out on somebody. We notice this flight doesn't have one MIG to its credit."

"Listen to the assassins," DeLeo said. "Don't talk too much before you know what it's like. You may end up wishing your mouth had been a little smaller."

Hunter reddened.

"Maybe," he replied.

That the flight had no claims, though, they were all conscious of. Robey's, in the room adjoining, was heavy with victories, eight altogether, Robey's five and three others. On the other side was Nolan's flight with four. Nolan had two of them. The contrast was marked for a flight between them with none. It was understood that Cleve had been installed to change this.

He finished putting his things away as well as he could and sat down on his cot. He was satisfied. He had a feeling of liking them all and of being liked. It was a rich infusion. They would make a name for themselves together. The opportunity to do that, to start fresh, from nothing, was everything he could have asked for. He retreated from reality as he considered it. He was not too concerned with how competent they were as flyers. He would make them good if he liked them well enough, if he loved them; and as they sat with each other in the darkening room about which winter hung, the confidence that he would find it all possible flooded over him. It was an effort to remain silent with this exhilaration inside him. It would all come in time, he was certain.

After a while they walked down to dinner together, passing by figures in the bleak evening that spoke out to greet DeLeo and Daughters. Cleve did not recognize any of them. The awkwardness of being a newcomer still nipped at him. They decided to stop at the club for a drink. The second lieutenants tagged along dutifully, although they did not drink anything stronger than beer.

The bar was crowded. Robey was there, sitting at a table with four or five others and rolling dice for drinks. They were still talking about his last kill, warming him with attention. He received it passively; but there was an aura surrounding him, a cloak of satisfaction. He had been transmuted. He was more than just himself, he was symbolic, as when the sleekness of his ship and the completeness of his equipment so enveloped him that, to a person as near as a wingman or far as a mechanic watching him climb out of sight, he inherited the beauty of his machine.

They sat at the bar. The room was small, and with the doors and windows closed voices crossed it easily. They could hear Robey among the others from time to time. DeLeo made an expression of distaste.

"Listen to that," he said, motioning with his head, "the ace, telling them all about it. That's what we'll have to listen to from now on."

"Maybe you can pick up some pointers," Daughters suggested.

"On what? Debriefing?"

"Let's call it enterprise. After all, he's made a name for himself."

"You bet he has. His mother wouldn't recognize it, either."

The lieutenants, one on each side of Cleve, were talking earnestly to him about when they could start their missions. They had both finished their training phase two days before.

"Do you think we'll get a chance to fly a mission soon, sir?"

"Maybe tomorrow."

"Tomorrow? For a fact now?"

"That's no promise. We'll see how things are."

"It's not easy to sit around and, well, you heard."

"Don't take it so seriously," Cleve said.

"I just want a chance to show certain people that maybe they were wrong about a few things, that's all."

"You'll get your chance."

"When I was freshman, we didn't mind stuff like this. Or in cadets. You expect it then."

"Where did you go to college?"

"The University of Texas."

Cleve nodded.

"They act like they own the war just because they've flown twenty or thirty missions," Hunter said.

"That's right," Pettibone added.

"What do they think we are?" Hunter complained.

"A couple of freshmen, I guess," Cleve said. "Three, actually. Minus the little caps."

"Oh, they won't try it with you."

"In a couple of months you'll be doing the same thing with the new boys. It takes a little while to become a veteran, that's all. Twenty or thirty missions, it looks like." He smiled inwardly as he said it. Desmond had been right. He was talking like one himself, already.

There was singing going on. Robey had organized three tables, and the room was flooded with noise which abated only slightly as they made the transition from one roaring favorite to another. Even DeLeo joined in. The songs were common property. When Colonel Imil entered, there were waves and shouts of acclaim. He stood grinning. His singing was confined to a mouthing of lyrics, but he always took part. It represented to him the qualities he liked to see in his pilots, and nothing was more important to him than they were. They made a wing, he claimed, and to have a great wing, one the glories of which would become legend, was Imil's honest objective. He allowed no other consideration, even selfish, to contend. In this respect he was a valuable commander. Everything was subordinate to the good of the wing.

He moved toward the bar and, seeing Cleve, stood beside him.

"What do they have you doing now, Cleve?" he asked.

"I took over a flight today."

"Damned good. How many missions have you got in?"

"Eight."

"It takes a few to get the idea," Imil confided, "but they tell me you're way ahead."

"I've only been in one fight."

"That has a lot to do with who you're flying with, but you'll be leading from now on. There'll be plenty of fights. All a man has to do is want to find them. You know what I'm talking about. That's all it takes. Christ, Cleve, we were flying together when all a fighter pilot ever had for breakfast was a cigarette, a cup of coffee, and a puke. You know what I mean. Now I have operations officers, for Christ's sake, and even a squadron commander, who don't have a MIG between them. Fighter pilots! But I'll take care of the real ones, Cleve. Good care. I always have, haven't I?"

One way or another, Cleve thought.

"You'll be getting that first kill," Imil said, pushing his glass across the bar for a drink. "It won't be long."

"I hope not."

"Don't worry. The desire, Cleve, that's all it takes."

More and more people were coming into the club as the riot of discordant song carried to the nearby barracks and the mess. They began to sit together by squadrons and to compete for volume, sometimes with two or three different songs going at the same time. Two of the squadron commanders were present, and the third had been summoned by telephone. A full drinking and singing bout was beginning.

"This is fine," Daughters muttered. "We haven't had anything like this since at least the night before last."

"Shut up and sing," DeLeo said, "or Imil will ground us all."

6

A chapping wind with a metallic tone to it was blowing. Excitement was present but subdued. At 1215 they rode down under the canvas of a truck lurching from every pothole. There was not much talking. The viscosity of the blood, Cleve thought, is changed. It actually seemed to be thinner.

There were coughs at the briefing and a constant shifting of feet. A pointer moved about the map, tapping the important locations, and every last detail of the mission down to the password at the front line was covered. The weather officer made wisecracks about the poor conditions up north. They filed out like men going to be inoculated.

"It'll be scrubbed," Daughters said.

Cleve agreed.

"I wouldn't be surprised," he said. "I think it's going to snow."

The sky looked gray and depressing. Hunter and Pettibone listened unhappily.

"But we've had the briefing," Hunter suggested.

"They'll scrub it, and we'll brief again," Daughters said. "It's all taken into consideration."

"What do you mean?"

"It's a hundred missions or a thousand briefings, whichever you get first."

At 1300 they were waiting in the locker room, the equipment hanging on them, loose and unzipped. Daughters was cleaning the inside of his oxygen mask with a handkerchief. Hunter and Pettibone sat together on one of the benches.

"What was that minimum fuel again? I swear I can't remember."

"Fifteen hundred pounds," Pettibone said.

"That's right. I keep forgetting. They certainly have a lot of figures for you." He glanced at Cleve and laughed apologetically.

"God, don't they?" Pettibone said.

"They didn't tell you the most important thing," Cleve said.

"What's that, sir?"

"Just get on my wing and stay there."

At 1325 they were in their ships, waiting. The minutes flickered by slowly. At last the chill whine of the first engines being started came through the air. They were definitely going.

At 1400 they were far beyond all memory of earth, near the Yalu, among great floes of clouds. They flew in silence. It seemed as if the war was over as they moved through the gray, deserted skies. Shreds of cirrus hung in the air, like icicles along the edge of a roof. The quiet was more ominous than clamor. They flew a track where the river might be, but any position was an approximation. They were unable to see the ground. The fuel gauge was the only reality as its needle retreated slowly from full internal load: twenty-six hundred pounds . . . twenty-five hundred.

At 1450 they were nearing home. It had been very significant for Hunter and Pettibone, but Cleve had little sense of achievement. As he landed, there was nothing but the emptiness of a wasted mission. White condensation poured from the tailpipes like steam when they shut down their engines. Individually, they trudged in toward the warm buildings.

At the debriefing it was definite that nobody had contacted MIGs. The greatest anxiety went then. It was not so bad after all. The failure was communal, and a sense of comradeship began to return.

Cleve walked slowly back to the barracks in the late afternoon. It had been a strange, lonely mission. Hunter had done all right, holding good position most of the time, saying something only when it was necessary, and then with rare brevity; but Pettibone, Cleve thought uncomfortably, was a little weak. He was either lagging or shooting ahead. He didn't seem to hear instructions. That was always a bad sign. Flying with him was like being responsible for a child in a crowd. He would require work and attention. He almost seemed to be in the wrong element, like a cat wading. Well, some developed more slowly than others.

The knob on the door to the room was loose. He had never been able to manage it with gloves on. He took the right one off and put his bare hand on the smooth, freezing brass. The door opened. He stepped gratefully from the cold into warm, shadowy comfort.

"Chung!" he called the houseboy.

"He's not here. I sent him out to get some blankets for me."

It was a stranger, a second lieutenant sitting on the sixth cot, his bags already unpacked. He was sorting through a file of papers, apparently straightening them out. There were several sheafs spread beside him. He offered his hand without standing up, as Cleve approached.

"I'm Ed Pell," he said, "but everybody calls me Doctor."

It was the pale lieutenant from Tokyo, the pursuer of waitresses. There was no mistaking those eyes. They were like acid.

"Have you been assigned to this flight?"

"That's what they tell me. How about you?"

"I've seen you before, haven't I? At Fuchu."

Pell regarded him closely.

"Maybe," he said. "I don't remember it though." He glanced at Cleve's name tag. "Connell?"

"Conn*ell*. I'm the flight commander."

"Good deal," Pell remarked calmly, rising to his feet.

It was all over him, the unfortunate wisdom of knowing enough to think he knew everything. Cleve could see that Pell was somewhat older than his fellows. It was to develop that he was twenty-five, and as free of idealism as a boy raised in the slums, although he actually came from open country in Michigan.

Cleve took off his winter flying jacket and then his pistol, lifting the harness from his shoulder and over his head. He tossed everything onto his cot.

"Just back from flying?" Pell inquired.

Cleve nodded.

"How did it go on the mission? Did you run into anything?"

"No."

Cleve sat down in one of the chairs near the stove and removed his shoes. The leather had become chilled and hard. He warmed his feet, massaging them with his hands as he did.

"Not a thing, eh?" Pell said, shaking his head sympathetically. "Tom."

"What?"

"Tom. You know, Captain, bad."

Cleve nodded slightly. The idiom was new to him. After a few minutes he put his shoes on again. He picked up a towel and some soap and stepped outside to jog to the showers, which were in another building. In the steamy room where taps branched out of rows of pipes running along the ceiling, he stood for a long time under the hot, devouring water. Warmth began to reclaim him, from the outside in, with delicious languor. He stayed until the skin on the tips of his fingers grew soft and puckered. Then he dried and dressed himself in another room, where two stoves maintained a good, high temperature. He returned to the barracks. Pell was gone. In the club Desmond was sitting at the bar.

"How was the mission, Cleve?" he asked.

"No good. All we saw was clouds."

"Did your new boys do all right?"

"There wasn't much they could do wrong. They didn't get lost anyway, which wouldn't have surprised me. One of them seems like a pretty good pilot, but I don't know about the other one."

"Pettibone?"

"Yes."

"I put a new man in your flight today," Desmond said after a pause.

"I know."

"Another second lieutenant. His name is Pell."

"Yes, I met him a little while ago. Have you talked to him?"

"Sure. He seems all right," Desmond said, "a little cocky maybe. They tell me that he's a good pilot, though."

"I hope so. He calls himself Doctor."

"What?"

"Says that's what everybody calls him."

"He'll be all right," Desmond assured him.

Cleve did not reply. Everything had changed somehow. It was like a passionate marriage suddenly palled by an in-law coming to stay indefinitely in the house. He fought a sense of disappointment.

It turned out that the three second lieutenants had been classmates all through flying school until they were separated before coming overseas. Pell was soon telling them what had happened to him since that time.

"You guys missed it. I came over on this Pan Am ship with a real babe for a stewardess."

"Don't give us that."

"I don't understand how it happened," Pell admitted, "but when we walked out to the plane in California, there it was, a big luxury job. The stewardess was smiling, and I said to myself, 'Doctor, this is an omen. Your luck is going to hold.'"

"It must have been pretty soft."

"Terrific. Hot coffee, sandwiches, reclining seats. The best." Pell picked a kiss from his lips with thumb and forefinger.

"I think we were pretty lucky to get assigned to this group," Pettibone said.

"You said it. I was really sweating back there at Fuchu. They held me up for ten days, trying to stick me in those lousy fighter-bombers."

"How did you get out of it?"

"Oh," Pell said, "I got to know the guy who was giving out the assignments. He finally fixed it up. What happened to everybody else in the class, though? Where did they go?"

"Let's see. Mullins, Boyd, Bechtel, and Tom Slazac went to fighter-bombers."

"The poor bastards," Pell commented. He had a lean, expressive mouth.

"They say they like it. They've already driven up here to see us once."

"What do they know about it? This is the deal."

"It surely is," Hunter agreed.

"Have you flown any missions yet? You probably have ten apiece, you weenies."

"We were on a mission this afternoon."

"Veterans, eh?"

Hunter shrugged.

"Have you seen MIGs yet?" Pell said.

"No."

"The weather was pretty bad today," Pettibone added.

"It was, eh? Tough."

Rummaging around in his belongings, he pulled out a full box of cigars and expertly slit the seal with a fingernail. He offered them around.

"How about one?"

Hunter accepted. Pettibone shook his head.

Pell picked out two for himself. He lit one and inserted the other in his shirt pocket. He was feeling more certain of himself.

"Have you run into any gin players around here?" he asked. "I'd like to find a game somewhere."

"How have you been making out?"

"Tom. I almost got cleaned in Japan."

"Don't tell me you lost."

"Not really," Pell admitted. "I managed to get well at the very end."

"Oh."

"I was playing with this old major. He had me way down, but the last couple of days I began getting to him and came out a little ahead." Pell grinned. He had a sly, condescending way of doing it.

"How much?" Hunter finally asked.

"Four bills, that's all."

"Four hundred dollars?"

Pell nodded.

"That's more than a month's pay. You didn't really win that much, Doctor."

"I didn't, eh?"

"Did you?"

"What's the difference? How about a quick game?" Pell said. "You and I?"

"No, I don't feel like it just now."

"Too bad," Pell said casually. "Well, I'll catch you some other time."

He stood smoothing his hair with his hand. Then he put on his hat and walked out. The door slatted shut behind him.

"Always some big deal," Pettibone muttered.

Hunter looked at the door without answering.

"Did you hear him?" Pettibone continued. "This is the place to be. He hasn't even been here twelve hours yet."

"He's something all right. Winning four hundred dollars. What do you think of that?"

"From a major," Pettibone said. "It had to be a major."

"That sucker knows how to play cards, though. I've seen him."

"So have I. Who cares?"

They glanced at each other in the darkened room, feeling the vague discomfort.

"He's the same old wise guy," Pettibone said finally.

Later, Cleve listened to Hunter obsessively describing Pell as a card player. He loved to gamble, and he was lucky. He always won. There was one night in Las Vegas when he lost eight or nine hundred dollars, and the club gave him cab fare to get back to the field; but then he came back and beat the blackjack game for over three thousand. Cleve did not doubt it. He had noticed Pell's hands. They were probably the most educated thing about him, thin and ascetic, with exceptionally long fingers.

"They must have been sorry they ever gave him the carfare," Cleve said.

The room had become confining for him, a regular closet. He stood up. He felt like a man who puts weight on a bad leg for the first time. Suddenly he was conscious of his position, uncomfortably. He was the leader. There seemed to be something artificial and repugnant about that, as if he were wearing a bright shirt with the word printed on it. Everything had been so effortless until now. Unexpectedly, the simplicity of things was gone. It had been a bad day.

7

Like the hand that bears the orb, the pilots—there were actually not many of them, about a hundred altogether—carried alone the ultimate strength of the wing. In each of the three squadrons there were some thirty, and in the rest of the structure perhaps fifteen others, who flew missions. It was a small complement; but even of the few there were only three who were recognized wherever they went: Imil, Bengert, and Robey. They stood out like men moving forward through a forest of stumps. Their names were gilded. They had shot down at least five MIGs apiece. Bengert had seven, but five was the number that separated men from greatness. Cleve had come to see, as had everyone else, how rigid was that casting. There were no other values. It was like money: it did not matter how it had been acquired, but only that it had. That was the final judgment. MIGs were everything. If you had MIGs you were a standard of excellence. The sun shone upon you. The crew chiefs were happy to have you fly their ships. The touring actresses wanted to meet you. You were the center of everything—the praise, the excitement, the enviers. If you did not—although nothing was shameful about it, and there were reasons, allegedly valid, for any man, no matter how capable and courageous, to have failed to get victories—still you were only one of the loose group in the foreground of which the triumvirate gleamed. If you did not have MIGs, you were nothing. Every day as he walked among them, Cleve knew it more truly.

Robey, of them all, was the most difficult to know. There was never any question of friendship; even a congeniality not much closer than that of two commuters was hard. Cleve made the effort. He had pride, but he forced himself. A drink at the bar, an occasional cool talk at night, always in Robey's room, it progressed slowly until one evening, unexpectedly, he found himself knowing Robey very well indeed.

He had walked in on a discussion of medals. A recommendation for Robey's third Distinguished Flying Cross had just been returned from Fifth Air Force Headquarters.

"I don't give a damn about the medal," Robey said. "I've got it already. I've got plenty of them. It's just the principle of the thing that smells."

The new policy was that Air Medals were to be awarded for MIGs destroyed, instead of DFCs, as had been done in the past. Robey was incensed.

"Next, they'll be giving merit badges," he said.

He had the rejected recommendation crumpled in one hand, and he smoothed it out as he talked. He had to refer to it while he rewrote it with the squadron awards and decorations officer, who was a lieutenant in his flight. They were modifying it.

"You have to make it sound like something for the Medal of Honor just to get a lousy DFC out of them," Robey said.

The citation had been matter of fact, reading simply "outmaneuvered the enemy aircraft with great skill." Robey was dictating a more stirring amplification.

"Although under fire . . . from one element . . . of MIG-15 aircraft . . . at the time," Robey said slowly as it was being copied down, "and in great . . . danger . . . better make that jeopardy; in great jeopardy . . . Captain Robey nevertheless pressed . . . a brilliant . . . timed attack . . . on another enemy element. Do you have that?"

"Wait a minute. Other . . . enemy . . . element. OK."

"And succeeded . . . in destroying the . . . lead aircraft . . . with a long . . . accurate burst . . . at a high angle off . . . and at . . . extreme range."

"All right. High . . . angle . . . off . . . extreme . . . range. There."

Robey picked it up and read it through.

"All right," he muttered. He could feel Cleve watching him. "That does it, eh?"

"It certainly does."

"This is ridiculous, isn't it?" Robey confided. "You'll find out though. If you want to get anything out of those desk pilots at Fifth, you practically have to squeeze it out of them."

"Is that what you're doing?"

"They won't turn this one down."

"I wouldn't know. Do you really think the DFC is enough, though?"

Robey's expression firmed, but he passed it off lightly.

"Hell, no," he said. "The way they make you fight to get one, there ought to be an extra medal to go along with it. For valor in the face of great administrative odds."

"I'd say you'd have earned that one."

"I wouldn't turn it down. I can tell you that."

"I don't see how you very well could."

Robey stiffened.

"I said I wouldn't."

Cleve got to his feet.

"I know," he said. "I've been listening to you."

"You've been talking mostly," Robey said. "As far as I can see, Connell, that's about all you do in that so-called flight of yours anyway. Why don't you go back and give them a few thousand words on what you think instead of trying to tell me?"

"I haven't told you what I think. I haven't even begun to tell you."

"Nobody asked you to," Robey replied.

DeLeo and Daughters were in the room when Cleve entered. He lifted one side of the blanket that covered the table and reached beneath it for the shelf where the mission whiskey was kept. It was issued at so many ounces per man per mission, but they usually received it in the form of two or three bottles to the flight, as a monthly dividend. He withdrew one and set it on the table.

"Jim?" he asked Daughters.

"No thanks, Cleve. Not for me."

He poured a drink for DeLeo without asking. His hand was shaking, and he moved so that he stood between them and the bottle. They mixed the whiskey with cold water from one of the canteens in the window box. Cleve sat back then and looked about him, at DeLeo, and at Daughters on his cot, sitting knees up, writing. He felt closer to them every day as their dimensions deepened for him, and at that moment especially he was sure he would have been lost without them. His so-called flight. Yes, they were that, he thought belligerently.

"Well, here's to the heroes," Cleve proposed. "Don't ever know one if you can help it."

"What does that mean?"

"I just spent a few pleasant minutes with Robey," Cleve said.

"So?"

He told them what had happened. When he had finished, DeLeo spit at the floor.

"That's for Robey," he said. "Don't let it bother you. If he's a hero, I'm a genius."

"He's a fighter pilot; that's something."

"Sure. It means he's a little crazy."

"Stop being a clown for a minute. He represents this—I don't know what to call it—craft. I use the word loosely. He's accomplished what he's supposed to do, he's shot down airplanes. If it was two or three, it wouldn't be so bad, but he's got five. He's not in the squadron any more, in a way. He belongs to all the fighter pilots, and if they're not so numerous, to anybody that might consider them. So there he stands. They look at him and see us, what we try to be. Robey, with his chest full of medals . . ."

"The medals?" DeLeo said. "They don't mean a thing. He could have a trunk full of medals and it wouldn't mean anything."

"Not to you, maybe, but you're a primitive."

"I'm a primitive? Just because I pick my nose?"

"That's the least of it."

"You're insulting everybody tonight, aren't you?"

Cleve smiled.

"Drink up," he said. "Don't be so sensitive. I only insult heroes."

Daughters went back to his letter.

After a while, Pell came into the room. He had been at the club with Hunter and Pettibone, and those two had gone to the nightly movie. They went religiously, no matter what was playing. Pell never did; there were too many other things demanding his time. At the moment, he was interested in meeting the nurses in the hospital down in Yongdongpo, and he'd arranged to borrow a jeep to go there the following night. His reputation of always having had great success with women was something that required constant renewal. He was intrigued by the prospect of a conquest under difficult circumstances.

Pell poured himself a drink and sat down at the table. He stirred the liquid with his finger. He seemed to be unusually contemplative.

"I'm in a rut," he complained. "Three missions, and I haven't been in a fight yet."

"You have a few left," Cleve said.

"Ah, the damned war may end any time, though. Did you hear the news broadcasts tonight? They've worked their way down to disagreeing on just one little point at the truce talks."

It was the first time that Cleve felt any shame himself at not caring whether it ended or not. There was a period of increasing pall. Pell had come, and the intimate mood had fled.

"Anybody feel like a few hands of gin?" Pell finally asked. "How about it?"

"No thanks," Cleve said.

DeLeo shook his head.

"What's wrong?" Pell complained. "Doesn't anybody around here play?"

There was a silence. Daughters folded the letter he had been writing and swung his legs to the floor.

"I'll play a few hands with you, Pell," he said.

He sat down at the table in his quiet way and watched as Pell picked up a deck of cards and began shuffling them with lean, expert fingers. He did not even seem to be aware of them whispering between his hands.

"What'll we play for?" Daughters asked unexpectedly. He was not given to gambling.

Pell lit a cigar, pushed his hat back, and slumped down comfortably in the wooden chair. He shrugged.

"Just make it easy on yourself, Jim," he said. "I don't care."

"How about half a cent a point?"

"Sure. That's fine with me. I don't want your money." He smiled. "I just need the practice."

Pell dealt out the hands quickly.

It started out as a fairly close game. Cleve sat watching it for about three quarters of an hour, surprised at how well Daughters was doing, and hoping for him. Compared with Daughters's gentle, almost resigned, attitude, though, everything about Pell's game was polished and cool. He seemed at least moderately pleased with every card he drew, and he discarded with confidence. He gave the impression of indeed only practicing. Daughters was a good player, but Pell seemed to have the luck when it counted, and that made the difference. By the time Cleve went to bed, Pell was winning more than twenty dollars.

8

When the ships returned from a mission, everybody watched for them. Usually, they came lining back to the field in flights of four, flying tight show formation with the black smoke fading in parallel streams behind as they turned in toward the runway and landing pattern. They seemed to be most indestructible then. They were of frozen silver. Nothing could possibly dim that grace. No enemy could deny them. Departures were stirring; but every return, even the most uneventful, was somehow transcendent and a call to the heart to rise in joy. Out of the north they had come again, brief strokes of splendor.

If they carried their drop tanks back with them, nothing much had happened on the mission. That was the first sign. If they came back without tanks, and broken up into pairs and occasional singles instead of fours, there had been a fight. As they trailed down the final approach and landed, it was possible to look closely and see whether or not the gun ports were blackened and the ship had fired. If many noses were black, it had been a big fight. The news of what had occurred on a mission often came from the radio monitoring in combat operations long before the planes were nearing the field, but not many heard it there. Most found out by watching the ships return.

Cleve had flown twenty-four missions. Except for his fifth on

Desmond's wing, he had seen no real action. They were always far off, going away, if he saw them, or overhead no bigger than flies, or sometimes as big as wrens; but to get up to them was like trying to jump off the ground and catch a bird—the altitude disadvantage meant that much. For a while he simply called it luck, but after too long a time of that there was nothing to call it. And there seemed to be nothing that he could do, no way to change things. He felt himself caught in a trough of despair. Day after day, unreasonably, he was on those missions that encountered nothing.

The evenings came early to end the short afternoons. Standing on the hill of barracks in the cold, with the watery sun almost down, he saw them returning from the late mission. The chill of the earth came through his feet and then edged up to make even his ears ache. His eyes wept from the wind as he watched. They were coming back in pairs. None of them had tanks. There had been a fight. An intense sinking feeling came over him. There was only one flight of four in the whole group. It hurt him to watch, and it was too dark to see their noses, but he waited stolidly through it as ship after ship came in, whistling smoothly down to meet the ground. The worst part, he knew, was what lay ahead, the empty hours of melancholy that would not be filled until he flew again. It was like the start of a relentless headache with its unavoidable hours of pain.

The word came, as it always seemed to, from nowhere. Cleve heard it as he walked down toward the line. A truck drove by, and somebody called out. Colonel Imil had shot down his sixth. Nolan had gotten another one. Four had been destroyed altogether.

The colonel was standing just inside the door of combat operations, smoking a cigarette, when Cleve saw him. His face was still half-mooned under the eyes where his oxygen mask had bitten into the skin. He was listening to the last of the mission reports.

"I heard you got another one, Colonel," Cleve said. His voice sounded flat to his own ears.

"That's right. How about you? Where were you anyway, Cleve?"

"I wasn't even on the mission."

"Why not?"

"I just wasn't scheduled, Colonel."

"Hell. You should have been there. They were everywhere today, some of them down at twenty-five thousand."

"Next time, I guess," Cleve said.

"Yeah. Maybe. You can't get them if you don't fly, though," Imil said, shaking his head.

Cleve did not reply. He fought down his pride and turned away. He knew what was happening. Even as an ordinary flight leader he was expected to get kills; but he had to live up to more than that. Everybody was watching him, many of them cynically. Everybody was waiting for proof of his ability, and somehow he had not been able to give it. He could sense the ebbing respect. It was showing up more frequently as the days passed.

He was overcome by a lonely, hopeless feeling. He did not want to talk to anybody, only to be by himself. Later, he might have a drink if the club was not too crowded, or perhaps even see the movie. Slowly the mood would abate, leaving finally only its invisible scar. Years ago, losing a football game away from home, he had walked like this, slowly, off the hard field, away from the crowd and the noise. The cleated shoes sounded hollow as they scraped down the long hallway to the locker room, and there were very few words that did not sound hollow, too. The ride home in the chartered bus seemed endless. Nobody talked, but only slept fitfully or stared out the cold, misting windows.

Perhaps it was true that through defeat men were made, and that victors actually lost, with every triumph, the vital strength that found exercise only in recovering strength. Perhaps the spirit grew greater in achieving the understanding that was first confused and then exquisitely clear after having lost. But that was, Cleve thought, like saying it was strengthening to be poor. It wasn't, he was sure. It was sapping. It was like having a leech's mouth on your breast, forever draining, so that everything had to be sacrificed for nothing more than sustaining the burden of flesh. There were very few men who ever surmounted poverty; and there were very few losers, he felt, who realized anything but tears from their defeats.

He wondered how this had happened to him, how despite himself he had been imprisoned by this inflexible choice of winning or losing; for there seemed to be no compromise between the two in this barren place where there was a single definition of excellence. If only there were some ground in between, some neutral stretch separating attainment and failure. He yearned for that. He felt emptied by desire. Suddenly he found himself wanting to be honorably relieved from the struggle, to have no part of it. Interminably, he saw it stretching out ahead of him, and he faced it with a sense of helplessness that he hated more than anything else. He had lost a moral independence. He had never lived without it before, and he did not know what to expect.

Whatever it was that had denied him the enemy, he wanted to meet and demolish. If it was only bad fortune, he could outwait that; but he was increasingly tortured by the thought that it might be something more insidious, he was afraid to identify what. If it was something unacknowledged within himself, then he was lost. The torment of that possibility tore at his heart.

He sat in the dark room, thinking. The clamor of Nolan and his flight returning to their room next door, shouting happily to each other and to those who came by to hear what had happened, streamed by him abstractly. At one point he was aware of Hunter's voice in there, but the actual words floated by him.

For a long time he sat quietly, in a solitude that gave only a vast discomfort instead of peace, pushing his thoughts before him as if through a jungle of spears. He was miserable. It could not go on. He had never been beaten, and it could not happen now; yet there was this before him which seemed to endanger everything he had fought for within himself. The mystic tissue that joined the soul of a man together, he felt it dissolving. He had to succeed. If he could only find them. He needed just a fragment of triumph, only that, to remove the doubts.

He did not know how many minutes or hours passed like that, but slowly his despair was washed away by visions, and he could see, as if it were reality, the enemy falling before him, hung on lengths of sailing tracers. He wanted only his chance, nothing more. Gradually he left the room, traveling with his dreams, heading as he always did to the same place, to the north with its silent seas of air, in which, if he lived, his victory had to be gained.

9

Major Abbott came around one evening in the long hour just before dusk. He was desperate to talk. There was an urging in him, a hunger, that was greater than he could bear, but it was difficult to say anything. Only a few inane phrases came at first. The houseboy stood by the window, motionless, staring out of it like a dog watching for birds.

"You get a few lousy breaks," he finally began, "and they're down on you. Everybody together. You might touch them or something. This fifty-cent war they're so proud of. My God, I was fighting a war, a real war, when they were taking grammar, most of them. Spelling!"

He had held it in for so long that it came out in painful fragments. He sat in his chair like someone applying for a badly needed job. It was impossible, but everything was being taken away from him. His life had been distinguished by only two things, his courage and his skill, but he had found them before he was very old, these precious stones, and when they were admired or spoken of he had known the fulfillment of owning the greatest prizes in the world. Suddenly, though, the past was being counted as nothing, like rescinded currency. What he had had for so long, what he had grown old in possession of, was gone now, sickeningly, and there was nothing else of importance to him, as with men who have given their lives to their children. It was all ended, the listeners to his stories, the crewmen eager to serve, the respect, the hundred happy terrors and ecstasies of height. He was alone, like a cripple facing the cruelty of running boys. They had no time for him any more as they tested their own keen nerve against each other.

"I'll be glad to get away," he said bitterly. "I just can't take any more, Cleve."

"You don't have a hundred missions."

"Fifty-one. And seventy in Italy last time. Seven kills. Six confirmed. Then you abort a few times because you've flown enough to know when a ship's not the way it should be, and the first thing, they think . . . oh, who gives a damn what they think, anyway."

"Why let it bother you? You're not finished yet. You have another fifty missions to get even."

"Not me. I'm going to Fifth. I'm all through with my missions."

"When?"

"Tomorrow."

"Seems pretty sudden," Cleve said.

"Not to me. I'd go tonight if I could."

"Who did it? Imil?"

"Yes. My old pal Dutch. He was careful to fix it up so that I was requested by Fifth." He laughed dryly. "To make it look good. To keep himself clean. I don't care."

"What will you be doing?"

"I'll be in operations. Not a bad job, either. A colonel's spot. Maybe even a promotion, just to rub in Imil's face a little."

"It's all for the best then, in a way."

Abbott looked up. He nodded his head reflexively, as if in time to some distant rhythm. He had looked everywhere for reason or relief, and sometimes he had been able to find it, temporarily, as when men achieve that stage of drunkenness at which they comprehend infinities. Suddenly his eyes filled with tears.

"Sure. It's really fine. Only I'd rather be a goddamned lieutenant flying wing, that's all," he cried, turning jerkily away. "I'd rather be dead."

Cleve took a quick, steadying drink of air. He was always embarrassed by nakedness. He seldom touched anyone physically.

"Carl," he began.

Abbott shook like a girl, with brimming, bottomless sobs. The houseboy stared out the window, never turning or seeming to hear.

It has to end some way, Cleve thought. He sat uncomfortably, with his reflections turned inward. The time came when you either did it yourself or it was done for you. Either way was hard. Prepared or unprepared, sudden or slow, it was all the same. Life stopped, and the world went on in the hands of others.

"I can't help it," Abbott said after a time, sighing unevenly. He kept his face turned. "You'll have to come down and see me in Seoul, when you get a chance."

"You'll be too busy briefing generals."

"No, I mean it. Come down."

"All right," Cleve said. He would have agreed to anything. He longed for a decent parting phrase.

"Any time," Abbott insisted. "You're the only one I can talk to."

That stayed in Cleve's mind afterward. He was reminded piercingly of school, where the athletes held to each other and the scholars strolled side by side. He hated Abbott for having said it; more and more as, with the maddening insistence of a nightmare, the days went on, cold and empty. They were the kind that, when looked back upon, seem indistinguishable one from another.

He started every mission with at least some measure of hope, but never was it realized. He was flying the day that Gabriel, the fourth flight leader in the squadron, who had come to the group after Cleve, got a MIG, but he saw nothing. He flew his twenty-eighth mission, his twenty-ninth, his thirtieth. His flight began to take some shape as an entity. Pell, it developed, was a good pilot who picked up experience quickly. He flew on a wing consistently well from the first, always in the right place, and his close formation was almost too close, a measure of insolence. Pettibone, in comparison, was uneven and would never get close enough. He seemed to meet an invisible barrier ten feet out. Cleve patiently guided him, never dwelling on more than one point at a time and as if incidentally.

"You have to anticipate more," he would say, "keep ahead of the ship. You're not doing that enough."

"I'm trying not to use the throttle too much."

"Stop worrying about that. That's a refinement. Use it all you want. Use it all the way from the gear warning to the fire warning light if you have to. That's what it's there for. Only use it in time, not when it's too late. Make the throttle your intention, not your reaction. You understand me?"

"I think so, sir."

"Good." It was slow work, but gradually it would come about.

One afternoon when Cleve did not go, Daughters led and got a damaged. Hunter had been on his wing; and that evening they listened as he enthusiastically described how it had happened, the first bit of mutual success. Cleve tried to feel happy, but it was poison to him. He felt, instead, as men do when they realize that they are losing their sanity, rational but overwhelmed.

When he sat in the briefings and looked at his name printed on the scheduling board at the head of his flight, he burned with self-consciousness. It seemed to stand out vividly beside the others: Nolan's for instance, Robey's, Imil's.

Finally, it was Colonel Moncavage who had no kills either, but then, on a single wild mission, got two. It was like an evisceration for Cleve when he heard it. Even Moncavage, he thought, somehow . . . At the bar the colonel took Cleve's congratulations smilingly, but soon turned back to Robey sitting beside him, to resume a narrative of how it had been accomplished. Cleve listened, feeling alien and empty. Robey was decorating the colonel's story with experiences of his own. There was nothing that Cleve could contribute.

"You should have gotten them long before this, Colonel," Robey said generously. "You just didn't have the breaks. Sometimes you have to wait for them, eh?"

"It certainly makes a difference when you have a couple," the colonel confided. "I was thinking I'd never have any luck. I finally see what you mean about getting them going away, too. I never would have gotten that second one if I hadn't reversed at the right time. He was just passing underneath me, and when I turned back I had a quick shot from less than five hundred feet."

The colonel swung around to Cleve.

"It only took one burst," he explained. "I still had over half my ammo when I got back."

"You must have waited until he was pretty close before you broke," Cleve said.

"Damned close."

"Another thing that's important," Robey interrupted, "is always take the last man in the formation if you can."

The colonel turned to listen to him, nodding appreciatively as he was told a story of how Robey failed to get a kill because he had not done that. Cleve left.

It was all unbelievable. Cleve was completely unaccustomed to the part he was playing, like a man who suddenly finds himself seriously ill. It was true, and he had to accept it, but it was somehow wrong, immensely so. His spirit was ebbing. He tried to present the same attitude he always had—even, capable; and though he was fairly successful in doing it, within he was broken. He had to consciously prevent himself from seeking sympathy or complaining. He said nothing. He kept it inside, where, like a serpent, it devoured him—heart, stomach, and soul. He devoted himself to his flight, working on Pettibone, encouraging Hunter, cautiously opening himself toward Pell. Meanwhile he lived on dwindling hope, always finding some for the next day somehow.

10

There came a morning like autumn or the long marble corridors of some museum. The sunlight seemed preserved as it gleamed from sleeping surfaces, and the air was still. They were on the second mission of the day.

"Great, Billy," Cleve told Hunter as they left the briefing and walked through the mild winter noon. "You've got No Go, and I have the Guzzler."

They were scheduled in one of the last flights and had been assigned the oldest, most troublesome ships. Hunter's was notoriously slow, and Cleve's drank fuel. Hunter laughed a little.

"This is the day that we're bound to run into a hundred of them," he said.

The previous mission had been in a running fight along the Yalu, but with no conclusive results. It was the first time that the MIGs had been up in several days, and there was a chance that they would be flying again this time, Cleve hoped.

"I'll be surprised if we just make it up there and back in those dogs," he said.

The locker room was never pleasant for Cleve. As they dressed, he felt the usual pre-mission discomfort. He was glib, but there was a looseness in his knees and the insistent uneasiness of what was he doing involved in all this? There was plenty of time to dress, too much time he had always felt. He talked with DeLeo and Pell, briefing them additionally. At last they all went out to the ships. Two members of a flight that was not going stood near the door as everybody left.

"Get one for me," they burlesqued.

The time before takeoff was always difficult, too. The mind could occupy itself, but the dumb, quavering heart could do nothing. Cleve sat in the cockpit, checking the second hand on his wrist watch. He drummed his fingers on the tight metal skin of the ship. Finally, it was time to start engines. He passed gratefully into the realm of function.

Once they were into it, the sky was clear, and bright sunny blue. It was a sky, Cleve thought, you could see tomorrow in. He looked over toward Hunter on his wing. DeLeo was flying number three, wide on the opposite side, just then moving into position with Pell number four out beyond him. They climbed north, over the quiet Haeju Peninsula and then across the edge of the Yellow Sea, heading the shortest way for Antung.

A fight seemed to have started already. They could hear the loud, excited transmissions of one flight among the MIGs. They were late, Cleve thought angrily. He pushed the nose of his ship down slightly, lowering the rate of climb and increasing the forward speed. He wanted to get to the Yalu as soon as possible.

At thirty-four thousand feet they began to leave smooth, persistent trails in the air. Cleve stopped climbing and dropped down several thousand feet to remain below the contrail level where they would be less visible. The river seemed deserted when they reached it. They could not locate the fight. Cleve asked several times where it was, but was unable to get any clear answer over the radio jammed with voices. He heard the ground control radar calling out train number four. There were many MIGs in the air, he knew, somewhere.

"Bandit train number five leaving Antung." In the tunneled voice of a stationmaster another one was announced. "Train number five leaving Antung, heading three five zero."

"Drop tanks," Cleve ordered.

He felt a buoyancy that was both fear and expectation. From here on, he was working against time to find them. He headed up the river, passing occasional elements, all friendly. He scanned the wide sky meticulously, high and low. There was a speck of dirt on the plexiglass canopy that looked like a distant airplane every time his eye passed over it. Despite himself, it tricked him again and again. Aside from that, there was nothing. As he turned to go down toward the mouth of the river he saw four ships chasing two MIGs far below, flashes of silver against the snowy ground. The radio was cluttered increasingly with cries of battle.

"Bandit train number six leaving Antung."

It seemed impossible to be traveling through so big a fight without finding anything. A desperate sensation of futility seized him. He was certain he was heading in the wrong direction, but he had turned less than a minute before. He could not cover ground fast enough. He felt as if he were merely hanging in air.

Someone called out sixteen MIGs heading south.

"Where?" Cleve asked.

No answer.

"Where are the sixteen MIGs?"

"Heading south! Sixteen crossing the river!"

"For Christ's sake, where?"

There was no answer.

Suddenly Pell called out something at three o'clock. Cleve looked. He could not tell what it was at first. Far out, a strange, dreamy rain was falling, silver and wavering. It was a group of drop tanks, tumbling down from above, the fuel and vapor streaming from them. Cleve counted them at a glance. There were a dozen or more, going down like thin cries fading in silence. That many tanks meant MIGs. He searched the sky above, but saw nothing. They were somewhere in that deep blue, though; they had to be. At great distances planes could appear and vanish before the eye as they turned or rolled out, depending upon the surface they presented, but these must be close. He had to see them. Segment by segment he checked and discarded the sky above. Then, from nowhere, there were two MIGs sailing past, headed the other way.

"There's two on the left!" Cleve called. "Let's go."

He turned—a delicate, speed-killing proposition at altitude—and fell in far behind them. It was another chase, long and useless, but they were going south. Sooner or later the MIGs would have to turn back. Cleve took a chance on that. He would never catch them otherwise, in the extended straightaway.

He looked back to check Hunter. DeLeo and Pell were not following. DeLeo called that he was breaking off to go down after some others. Cleve could not see them. He looked forward again. A moment later the MIGs he was trailing started a wide, climbing turn. It was sooner than he had hoped for. He cut to the inside, gaining on them.

"You're clear! You're clear!" he heard Hunter calling.

They continued to turn. He drew nearer. It all seemed childishly simple. He wondered if they had seen him yet. He was almost in range, closing on the second MIG steadily. He ducked his head to see the gunsight reflection on the armor glass. The MIG was growing bigger and bigger in the bright reticle.

"Keep me cleared."

"You're all right."

Before he could fire, the MIG banked steeply and tightened the turn. He's seen us, Cleve thought. The limber sight computed itself off the glass screen as Cleve turned hard after him. The MIG began to climb. The sight swam back into view. Everything seemed to be going at a sleepy pace. They were not moving. They were all completely motionless in a glacier of space. The leader had disappeared. There was just this one. He fired a brief burst. The tracers lined out and fell short, like a bad cast. He pulled the pipper forward a little as the MIG turned, still climbing. He squeezed off another burst. It fell around the wing. He could see a few flashes there and the minute debris of glancing hits. He managed to move the pipper forward again, leading more.

"There's one coming in on us," Hunter shouted. "We'll have to break."

"OK," Cleve said, "tell me when."

"It's two of them."

With just a few grains of time he could do it. He had no thoughts but those that traveled out on a line of sight to the plane ahead of him. He needed only seconds. He fought the impulse to look behind. The pipper refused to stay in the right place. He kept calmly adjusting, holding his fire. It was like standing on the tracks with his back to an express already making the earth tremble. He fired again. A solid burst in the fuselage. The silver lit up in great flashes of white. He was playing a machine in a penny arcade. Suddenly he saw something fly off the MIG. It was the canopy, tumbling away. A second later the compact bundle of a man shot out.

"Did you see that, Billy?" he shouted.

"Break left!"

Cleve turned hard, straining to look back. Two MIGs, firing, sat close behind. Their noses were alight. He was turning as hard as he could, not gaining, not yet feeling himself hit, thinking no, no, when at the last moment they were gone, climbing away, in the direction of the river.

Cleve saw nothing more of the fight. He headed north for a while, but it had all ended. There was only the meager conversation of flights withdrawing from the area. It was over. The fight had dissipated. The MIGs were gone.

Cleve had never felt so fine as when finally they headed back through the quiet sky. This was the real joy of it all. He understood at last. He looked across at Hunter. His ship, far out, was like a silver, predaceous minnow with an abrupt, featherish tail. It seemed to be fixed against the azure blue of altitude. At that moment, Cleve could not remember ever having doubted that he would know this heady, sweet surfeit. Instead, it was just as he had always felt it would be. He knew then that he would never lose.

He was unprepared for what happened soon after they had landed. He thought he heard a crew chief say it, and then they told him as they walked to debriefing: Pell had gotten one, too. Cleve saw DeLeo waiting for him outside the sandbagged operations building. He appeared angry, tight with fury.

"What happened, Bert?" Cleve asked.

"Haven't you heard?"

"They tell me that Pell got a MIG."

"That's right. The son of a bitch went off alone and got one."

"Alone? By himself?"

"Sure, by himself," DeLeo said.

"He didn't say anything to you?"

"Not about leaving me. I was going after a flight of four of them. It was after we left you, later, and he called that he had some more of them out to the side of us. I said OK, and the first thing I knew he was gone, and I had two right in back of me that I damned near never got away from."

Pell came up, his face circumspect, but subduing a grin.

"How'd it go?" he said to Cleve casually. "I understand you got a MIG."

"That's right. I hear you got one, too."

"I did," Pell said happily. "I guess I was pretty lucky. I got hits all over him, though."

"Where did you get the idea that you could take off alone in the middle of a fight?"

Pell's expression was innocent.

"I didn't know I was alone," he protested, "until I was just about to start firing on this MIG, and then it was too late to do anything else. I lined up behind him . . ."

"What do you mean you didn't know you were alone?" Cleve interrupted. "What made you think you could go off and leave your leader?"

"He said it was OK. I asked him."

"Listen, you son of a bitch," DeLeo began, "you never asked me a thing."

"Yes, I did. I called out two MIGs to the right of us, and you said it was OK to go after them. I thought you were with me all the time."

"I didn't tell you to go after anything," DeLeo said flatly.

"I thought you did. Well, that's probably what caused us to become separated."

"I don't care what caused what, Pell. You never said a word to me, and even if you did, I didn't tell you anything about going after them. When you're flying wing, your job is to cover me, and you stay there and do that no matter what you see or think. You almost got me killed today."

Pell did not reply.

Cleve was tempted to let it go as a misunderstanding. Things like that could happen easily enough in the excitement of fighting, he reasoned. Meanwhile, it seemed as if a dozen people were crowding around him, offering handshakes and asking how he had done it. He found it difficult to sustain any displeasure. He was swept along in a flurry of rejoicing. There were two MIGs in his flight.

"Cleve," Imil said, punching him on the flat of the shoulder, "I knew you'd do it. It took a while, but I knew you would."

"He bailed out," Cleve grinned. "I could have kissed him."

"You should have given him a squirt."

"Oh, no. That one's my friend. He may be back tomorrow with another MIG for me."

Imil laughed.

"It's only the beginning," he said. "You're on the way now. I hear a wingman in your flight got one, too."

"That's right."

"Who was it?"

"Pell. He's a second lieutenant."

"Pell, eh? They tell me it was only his seventh mission at that. Well, that's good work."

Everybody was saying nice going. Nolan came by, and Desmond. The debriefing was continually interrupted. A sergeant was standing by to take pictures for press releases. Cleve felt the full warmth of exhilaration devouring him. So this was what it was like to win. Already he could no longer recall the hunger and despair of days past.

DeLeo stood in the background silently. Cleve took the opportunity to talk to him as soon as he could. He wanted to smooth it over.

"It won't happen again," he said.

"He's going to get shot down," DeLeo swore. "They'll get him up there alone and murder him. He's a smart one, but I don't care how smart he thinks he is or how good he thinks he is. If he's alone, he can't cover himself, and they'll get him. I don't give a damn if they do. He's asking for it. He'll never leave me again, though. I won't fly with him."

"He's all right," Cleve argued, feeling the words awkward in his mouth. "It was probably a misunderstanding, that's all. Give him the benefit of the doubt."

"It was no misunderstanding."

"It might have been. Those things happen."

"Who do you believe anyway?" DeLeo asked. "Me or him? It has to be one of us."

"It's not a question of that."

"It's not, eh?"

"I'm just trying to bring out that it could have been an honest mistake."

"Honest?" DeLeo said. "He knew what he was doing."

"We'll see."

They stood there for a while close to one of the flat, interior walls of the quonset, not talking. Pilots still thronged about the map-covered tables, explaining what they had done and seen, and the room was filled with voices. Cleve caught sight of Colonel Imil talking to Pell near the doorway. The colonel seemed happy. Pell must have been elated, too, but his expression was composed, a smile both modest and assured.

Hunter came by. He was brimming with words and excitement.

"You should have seen it," he told DeLeo. "MIGs in front. MIGs in back. It was a circus."

He turned to Cleve. "I still don't know how we got away with it," he said.

"You played it just right, Billy."

"Oh, no," Hunter cried. "You were the cool one in there. I was scared. I admit it. I was keeping my eye on the ones behind, though. I was trying to judge it just right. You know, the last second, like you said."

"You were perfect. I mean it."

"It worked out, didn't it? Just right. We'll get them again, too."

"You bet we will, Billy." Cleve was grinning.

11

For a time, everything was good. He was light, almost frivolous with satisfaction. He walked against the bitter wind, along roads frozen into stone, with a feeling that all of it was his dominion, bleak but his own. His name had some meaning. Moving among the others or alone, he was again and again conscious of victory. He had found himself. It was easy to laugh and nothing to smile. He hardly felt it wearing thin until suddenly it had happened, like an awakening after a night of love.

It was five days later that he sat listening to a mission in combat operations. Colonel Moncavage was leading it. Half an hour before, it had taken off in a dawn as calm as a sea of glass. Four of his flight were on it: DeLeo leading, Pettibone, Daughters number three, and Pell. The weather briefing beforehand had indicated it would be nothing more than a milk run. North Korea was heavily clouded over. In addition, they were flying to provide escort for a photo-reconnaissance ship, and those missions seldom developed into anything. Cleve stared through the window at the sky. He could see only small portions of it through the stratus decks. It was a dull, chilly morning, streaked with a grittiness that made all conversation seem stilted. His mind wandered to the thousand other places that life could have taken him to instead of this one.

He listened to the curt radio transmissions. The familiar ominous feeling that he could not quell grew within him. He wished he had gone himself. Nothing specific had caused it. That was the way he always felt. It was the old recurring apprehension. Whenever they went off without him, he was certain he had made a mistake. He could not be on every mission, however; it was a question of picking the right ones. But he sat nervously, for no reason that he could isolate, other than a deap-seated doubt.

It was like an alarm sounding when he heard them report the target area being relatively clear. No clouds. He should have known it. The damned forecaster was wrong half the time; if he said fair, it was likely to flood. The fear of having decided badly grew stronger. He waited uncomfortably. Now he was in for half an hour or more of sickening suspense.

He stood up and wandered about the room, trying to occupy himself. He looked over the maps on the walls again, the rows of charts, the claims board. The last he stood before for some time. On it was listed the name of every pilot in the group who had ever had a confirmed claim in Korea. Small red stars marked them. There were separate columns for aircraft destroyed, probably destroyed, and damaged, but it was only the first column that really counted. His eye moved down the trail of names. Many of them he did not recognize. They had left the group long before. Some belonged to dead men. There was Robey's, with five stars after it. Nolan had three. Bengert, seven. Imil, six. Tonneson had thirteen, two full lines on the board. And there was his own name with one, and Pell's. Cleve had seen men come in every day to glance at this board and admire their names on it. It was the roll of honor. Hunter had once told him that he would rather have his there than anything else in the world. It was absurd, and yet impressive. Anything that men would willingly die for had to be considered seriously. From this board, perhaps, or one like it, could come names a nation would seize in its appetite for heroes. For a truly singular record there might be lasting fame.

Abrupt voices interrupted his thoughts. They had seen something up north. Cleve moved quickly to the radio. He turned up the volume.

". . . at twelve o'clock, Blue Lead," somebody said.

"Roger, I have them."

"Four more at ten high."

It was garbled for a moment. They were all talking at once.

"They look like MIGs."

"I don't have them now."

"One o'clock! One o'clock!" someone called.

There was brief, unbearable silence. Then, "They're MIGs! Drop tanks, Blue."

The air filled with voices blocking one another out. He heard other flights cleaning up their airplanes and joining the fight. He had a sensation of drowning, of everything starting to go the wrong way. He felt a terrible impotence. The transmissions overlapped crazily. It was difficult to follow what was happening, but somebody had gotten one. He heard a sharp call:

"He's bailing out! There goes the chute!"

He sat quietly, overcome with depression. He tried to rationalize: it was over so little, like a child who has not been invited to a party, brooding. Nothing would help him, though. He listened in despair. The cries of those triumphant beat on him like waves of nausea.

Colonel Imil came in. He frequently dropped by to check on a mission's progress if he was not flying himself.

"Hello, Cleve," he said. "How's it going up there?"

"Terrible."

"What do you mean? What's wrong?"

"Nothing. They're in a fight."

"A big one?"

"It's hard to tell, Colonel. It sounds pretty big."

"They get any?"

"One at least," Cleve said. "Maybe more."

"Nothing wrong with that."

They sat listening together, but not much came over the air. The fight had already begun to dissipate. Like a storm, it was preceded and followed by incongruous calm. The colonel tried the volume control. It was full high.

"It must be over already," he said. "Do you know who got them?"

"Couldn't hear."

"Who's flying?" He walked over and read a scheduling board. He grunted. "Nobody much. Maybe Moncavage did some good. He's got a chance with that line-up, anyway."

"Maybe," Cleve said. "My flight is up there."

"Which is that? DeLeo?"

Cleve nodded.

"I can't place him right off. He hasn't done much, has he?"

"Not yet."

"Is he any good?"

"If he gets the chance."

"Well, we'll see. Maybe this was it for him."

"He's due."

Imil gestured toward the claims board.

"That's what I judge by," he said. "That's where it shows. You talk about chances. Look at that, Tonneson for instance. Thirteen kills. That's not like winning a lottery. Nobody can convince me that he just had thirteen chances while some other guy had none. What he did have was the urge to go a little farther than anybody else was willing to, maybe not thirteen times, but most of them. There it is, right on the board."

"Yes. Of course, he was somewhat above average as a pilot, too."

"Oh, sure. He was good. The big thing, though, was that little extra courage and pride. That's what makes the difference."

"I suppose so."

"I know it," Imil emphasized. He paused. "Sometimes the ones who've got it don't realize how important they are, how much things depend on having enough men with just that little more. I mean it, Cleve."

"Yes, sir."

The colonel stood there reflectively, rapping the counter lightly with his knuckles. Suddenly the radio began again. Moncavage's voice was recognizable. The first flights were heading back. Imil listened for a minute and then picked up the microphone and called.

"Go ahead. This is Red Leader," Moncavage replied.

"Hey, Monk, this is Dutch. How'd you make out?"

"Say again."

"This is Dutch, Monk. How many did you get?"

"Four, I think," Moncavage said.

"Who got them?"

"I don't know yet. Not me, anyway."

Cleve stared at the floor. He heard the colonel put the microphone down.

"They got four," he announced happily to the intelligence and weather officers who stood in the doorway, the clerks behind them.

"They'll be getting back in about twenty minutes," the colonel continued, looking at Cleve. "Let's go out and watch them land."

They drove out to the runway and parked beside the control truck. They did not have long to wait. Soon afterward, the first ships began to return and enter the landing pattern. Cleve watched them streaking in on the initial approach against a background of pearl-shell clouds that seemed to accelerate them, like trout crossing a bright brook bottom. They were all elements of two, with occasional singles. As they came in over the end of the runway to land, the dust puffed up behind them. He looked closely when they swept by him, reared with their nose gears still held off the ground. He did not see many that had fired. He listened and watched for his own flight as more and more ships appeared, school-like, around the field. Finally, he heard them. They had been split up like the rest. Daughters and Pell came in first. They broke almost directly overhead. He watched them fly the pattern. Their gear came down. They turned onto the base leg. Then they were banking steeply on the final turn and dropping fast. One close behind the other they settled in on the runway. Cleve could see it from far off. It was as if he had known beforehand that it would be. Pell's gun ports were carbon black.

It was true. When they drove in after the last ships had landed, they heard that Pell had gotten another MIG. He had seen it, very low, heading along the Yalu on the deck. He'd called it out to Daughters, but Daughters had not been able to spot it and told Pell to take it. Pell did, going down all the way from thirty-five thousand feet. At the last minute, he saw there were two MIGs and that he had misjudged and was going to overshoot; so he'd started firing from far out of range, holding the trigger down as he closed, and had managed to spray in enough hits so that the pilot ejected himself just as they flashed past.

"Pell got another one," Colonel Imil said. "That boy must be really hot. He's the one in your flight, Cleve, isn't he?"

"Yes, sir."

"He's a comer. He'll be one of our next aces."

Cleve said nothing. He was experiencing a sense of imprisonment. He felt a deep yearning to be outside, where he would not have to hear about it.

Desmond had been on the mission, too.

"What do you think of your boy now?" he asked Cleve.

"Pell?"

"I told you he was going to be good. Remember?"

"I remember, all right."

"He did a fine job this morning."

"Yes," Cleve said. "He can fly. I may be wrong about the rest."

"I think you are."

"We'll see. It won't be the first time."

He walked to where his flight stood around a table, giving its account of the mission.

"Hey, Cleve," Pell grinned, "you missed a good one. You should have come along."

Cleve did not answer. He took Daughters aside.

"How did it happen?" he asked.

He wanted to hear a first-hand account. Daughters told him the same story he had heard already.

"I don't know how he ever spotted him," Daughters admitted. "We were down to twenty thousand before I saw him. That Pell has a pair of eyes."

It came to that, time after time, who could see the farthest. Cleve was determined not to submit to it. He argued automatically: "He might have caught a flash of sun on him."

"I don't think so, Cleve. I believe he can see a bird's nest from forty thousand. I really do."

The furor of debriefing was at its peak. It had been a big morning, and excitement ran high. Everybody was anxious to find out the details of what had happened, or to make their claims. Shouted congratulations crossed the room. It turned out, when the fragments of the fight had been consolidated, that five MIGs had been downed altogether. The reconnaissance ship had not gotten its photographs. The enemy had been up in such strength that Colonel Moncavage had ordered the photo ship to turn back; but it had been a great victory, despite the abandonment of the original mission. Five kills and no losses. Cleve stood listening to the undercurrent. Everybody was talking about Pell: a second lieutenant, a wingman, with two kills. It was an extraordinary achievement.

"It had to be him," DeLeo said mournfully. "Christ. Now we suffer."

"Daughters thought he was pretty good," Cleve said.

"Daughters is probably covering up for him."

"He's not. I talked to him."

"Just between us," DeLeo said, "Jim is a fine type, but he ought to be back teaching school somewhere. I know Pell. I've seen dozens like him. The wise ones. Where I come from, they end up in alleys, on their faces. Either the cops or the big boys take care of them. Pell's one. You're not going to change that."

"How about giving him half a chance, Bert?"

"I already have."

Cleve smiled mirthlessly.

"You're a tough one," he said.

In the mess hall that noon, Pell sat with Hunter and Pettibone, telling them about the fight. They listened absorbed. They were not eating, but Pell was, hungrily, as he described the action.

"I was lucky as hell," he said confidentially. "That pass I made on him: tom. Strictly tom. If I hadn't gotten him that first time, either he or his wingman would probably have gotten me. I really hit him good, though. You should have seen the flashes. He lit up all over. Then, just as I went by him, pouf!"

Pell exploded his fist into fingers. That was the pilot going out.

"That was good shooting, Doctor," Hunter said.

Pell flicked his hand in a dispelling gesture to show how difficult it had been.

"I just hosed him from three thousand feet all the way in," he explained. "I was closing too fast to do anything else. I can't wait to see the film, though. If it comes out, it'll be terrific. I told those boys in the photo lab to take special care of it."

"How come Daughters didn't get the second MIG?"

"Daughters?" Pell laughed. "He's lucky it didn't get him."

Throughout the meal they were stopping at the table to say something to Pell, to pay their respects. Many of them were merely curious, and a few were seeing Pell for the first time. It was not a ritual, but there was a certain formality involved. The words were always the same. The tone was reserved. Hunter and Pettibone sat quietly through it, watching with envy and also—they could not resist it—pride. They were wingmen together, in the same flight. Regardless of what happened, he was one of them, and he had shown them hope.

12

The next morning there was rain and a low ceiling. It was the beginning of a spell of bad weather. There were days of no flying whatsoever. Time passed slowly or seemed to have stopped. Through the dismal, dragging afternoons they sat, waiting for the sky to appear once more. In the cell-like rooms they read or talked, the radio playing incessantly. It was like a succession of Sunday mornings in a small town. The hours of idleness were long. In the beginning, Cleve was able to endure them, but inactivity was a relentless grinding stone. A few days of it in a row could bring the calmest man to touchiness and irritability.

There were a few isolated missions, but in marginal weather and through shrouded skies. There were never any sightings. Things seemed dead. It was a time of unreality, and expectations quickly disappeared, like a bet compounded on a dice table and then suddenly lost. It was hard to remember fair days, nor did it seem that they would ever come again.

Once they went in haze that made it like flying through yesterday, until finally, on top, it was as flat as a table at thirty thousand and the horizon was rimmed with a band of green mist. They wandered this plateau in long, straight legs, encountering nothing. Coming back, out over the water, the haze was thinner, and slick patches of it far below looked like gilded mirrors as the sun hit and penetrated them.

There was a mission when they conned across seas of eternity, never catching sight of the ground except at the beginning and end. There was another when, halfway north, near Pyongyang, they heard in their earphones the high whine of what seemed to be gunlaying radar. The radio picked it up by some fluke. There was the thin tone of it, searching back and forth and then suddenly locking on and following them through the intervening clouds until they were out of range. It was a lone message from earth, and the sound of destiny, too, Cleve thought, tracking his path through even the quietest of flights. From all of these they came home at last, low on fuel and unsuccessful.

Billy Lee Hunter was depressed. He sat talking to Cleve one dark afternoon. It was raining outside. The sound of it on the panes of glass was like blowing sand. He didn't know, Hunter said. Everything was wrong. He supposed he was just not the type.

"Not what type?"

"Oh, you know," Hunter explained. "The Doctor is the type."

"Jesus Christ," Cleve muttered.

"What?"

"Just Jesus Christ. Is that all that's bothering you?"

"It's this weather, too."

"We'll get good weather. Spring will be here soon."

"I suppose so. I wonder if it will make any difference, though. Sometimes I think I'll never see them, no matter what happens."

"We'll see plenty of them when the weather breaks."

"Do you really think so?"

"Sure."

"It's all these stories about MIGs being shot down. They read them at home; my dad reads them and wonders why I haven't done anything here."

"If your dad thinks it's so easy to do," Cleve said, "tell him to come over and try it himself."

"You don't understand. He's always been proud of me."

"Well, you'll make him proud. Stop whining about it." Cleve was sorry the moment he had said it.

"Listen here"—the Texas honor had been impinged upon—"I don't whine. No, sir."

"Sorry. I didn't mean that. I know you're not whining."

There was a recuperative silence.

"Just stick with it," Cleve continued. "Things will work out. For all of us. You don't think I like it any better than you do?"

"No. I guess not. I just get discouraged."

"Don't worry, Billy. You'll get your chance."

"I wish I knew that."

"You will."

"I'll probably muff it anyway when it comes."

"No, you won't. You're the least likely to muff it of anybody in the flight."

Hunter looked at him with surprise.

"I mean it, Billy."

He was a good man, childish and courageous. He reminded Cleve of prep school, when everything had been in moral primaries, and life had seemed as clear as a biography. Hunter's world had no vague pastels. It was bounded sturdily by boyhood, grandfatherhood, the Bible, and the Cotton Bowl game. And yet Cleve could not do anything but admire an honest man, no matter how simple. Hunter was a good pilot, too. He had come along quickly. He would be leading elements before long and flights before he was finished. He was considerably better than Pettibone, who still did not seem able to extend himself beyond merely staying in formation; and he was certainly as good, though not as aggressive, as Pell. Hunter was reliable. That was the quality for a wingman. In the end he would accomplish more than Pell. Cleve would see to that. It was a responsibility almost, and he wanted to fulfill it. He vowed to.

"We'll each get one before long," Cleve told him.

"I wish I could count on that. I surely do."

"You can. We'll get them."

Cleve sat thinking about it, smoking a cigarette and watching the smoke fall to the ceiling in a blue, distending spire. He stared outside at the raining sky. It could not last much longer. The weather had been miserable for over a week. It would have to improve soon.

In vain, though, they waited. They watched the sky through dismal days. It was never blue. It was like a layer of grief. Almost unnoticed, because it brought no change, the spring started like this. The weather remained sullen. The rain fell drearily from swollen skies. It seemed as everlasting as surf. It came first hard, then soft, like layers of gravel. The slate roofs gleamed beneath it. Dirty streams of water coursed the roads, and the floors of every building were muddy from clodded shoes. Frogs appeared, legions of them. From the cold exile of winter, they returned with a vengeance. The croaking, especially at night, filled the air. In the evenings the club was loud with insane, continuous partying. It was on such a night that Cleve and DeLeo decided to go to Japan for a few days of leave. The idea was like finding a coin in the mud. Nothing was happening anyway, and the weather showed no sign of breaking. It was a perfect time to get away. Cleve was enthusiastic.

Daughters agreed at first to go along, but then in the morning he changed his mind and decided against it. He was too close to finishing, he said. He had more than eighty missions, and he wanted to stay and fly the rest as quickly as he could, even if he only got in one or two during the time he might have been away. A delirium of home, not so far off now, had seized him. He had written to his wife that he hoped to be back before the summer started. The fever was on him, the unbearable longing for home and love that came when the end was near. It was irresistible. At the last he would be moving toward it, heedless of everything else, like a man making his way to an exit in a fire.

Cleve was elated, however. He felt as if a great holiday were at hand. The night before their departure for Japan, he convinced DeLeo that they ought to drive into Seoul for a steak dinner.

"To condition ourselves," he explained.

Daughters went with them, and they left just after dark. It was the first time Cleve had traveled the road into Seoul since the day he had arrived. Though rougher and more uneven than he remembered, it gave him a strange sense of freedom to be going back over it, away from duty and its demands. Seoul was shattered. There was no traffic on the damp streets. A few weak yellowed lights shone from windows. It seemed a ghost city, with miles of empty trolley tracks threading the gutted shells of buildings stripped of all glass and wood. The wide avenues were like a sour-smelling trip through antiquity.

The bar at the Fifth Air Force club had been some sort of shrine. On three sides were double doors adjoining each other, which served instead of walls, but these were opened only in warm weather. The wood was carved ornately and gilded. Mirrors multiplied the effect. It was like sitting in a huge jewel box, and there was a large crowd in a variety of uniforms. They ordered champagne. Outside, the rain began to fall.

"Listen to that."

It sounded like a sheet of water waving before the wind. The gusts were as clear as if they could be seen.

"Come to Japan, Jim," Cleve said. "The weather won't be any good here."

"Pour me some more champagne."

"I'll pour you all you want. How would you like a bath in champagne in Tokyo?"

"It's not high on my list. Sounds more like Bert."

"Come on with us in the morning. We'll have a time."

"The weather may break. I only have nineteen missions to go. I want to finish up. Besides, I'm married."

"Not in Tokyo."

"I can't go, Cleve."

"Have some more champagne."

They drank a second bottle. The rain had begun to abate. There was only the thin sound of it, like a hiss, and through that the musical, heavy drops falling from the roof. At the next table someone was complaining about how tough the briefing for General Breck had been that day. The general had been in an ugly mood. He had not even bothered to light his cigar.

"Cleve!"

It was Abbott, calling as he edged through the tables toward them. He was followed by another major. They came up to the table.

"How have you been?" he asked, smiling.

"Fine. What about you?"

"This is purgatory," Abbott said. "I stoke fires with paper all day long."

He introduced the major who stood beside him.

"This is Ben Gross. He works with me in this pest hole." They sat down. "Well, you got yourself a MIG, Cleve, didn't you?" Abbott said.

It was nice to hear somebody saying that. Cleve nodded.

"That's the hardest one, that first one," Abbott continued.

"Can you guarantee that?"

"That's what they say. How did it happen?"

"Oh . . ." Cleve began.

How did it happen? Abbott had asked. What did it matter to him now, but he had to know. His heart was still far away from here, wedged in the cockpit, waiting to go north again. His heart was beating like a fish in a net, miles up in the thin air over Sinuiju. Abbott made no pretense of being at home in these surroundings. He sat awkwardly in his chair, as if perched, like a caged wild bird. His friend, the other major, he seemed to have forgotten in a moment. He was with old comrades now. Everybody else was a stranger. Everything else fell away like cloth before fire.

"How did it happen, Cleve?"

"He just got in my way."

"No, really."

He had to know. It was news from what had been home, and he was famished for it, like an exile. He was a man lost, afloat on foreign tides. He could never return, nor would he find peace where he was. There was nothing he could do but exist on memories and seize upon an old friend passing, with the grip of a dying man.

It was painful to see. Cleve felt it in his stomach like an iron egg. It was like watching a man hanged. He could feel the rope about his own neck, his own hands lashed, his knees gone. It could be happening to him too easily, to anybody who loved too fiercely or was true to what he believed. He could see himself in Abbott's place, sitting across the table, devouring the crumbs he was lucky enough to find. He did not want to look, but the compunction was as strong as that of taking a last glance at the wax face of a friend lying in state. Perhaps that was why they all hated Abbott, Cleve thought, because they saw themselves.

He could not get away from it, even for an hour. There was a way to live and a way to die. He was supposed to show them that. It was what you had to demonstrate to be a leader. At moments like this he was certain that he was miscast. He did not have enough to give. He did not love men enough.

If he did have a failing, it was excessive lucidity, which can be the same as blindness. He should have been aware. DeLeo was proud, but not beyond yielding. He would have crawled for Cleve. Daughters was afraid, but he would have concealed it. The leader does not know he is their saint. He does not hear what they say about him. He feels his loneliness and does not recognize its meaning. He looks forward and does not see them following. He falls and does not know they have triumphed.

". . . heavily outnumbered by enemy fighters," Daughters was saying, improvising a citation for Cleve's story, "through curtains of flak, and the most adverse weather conditions, in the highest traditions of the United States Air Force."

"All pilots will report to wing headquarters," DeLeo added, "to receive medals. If you have one, draw one. If you have two, turn one in."

They had another bottle of champagne after the majors left. By the time they were ready to eat, it was too late. The kitchen had closed. It was a fine evening despite that. They drove home after midnight, through a dark, exhausted city and along empty roads, singing most of the way. It had stopped raining. The night was cool and mild. The moon shone through thin clouds that looked like a layer of wet newspaper.

"Tokyo tonight," DeLeo grinned.

"Tomorrow night, you mean."

"This is tomorrow."

13

It was drizzling again in the morning when they flew out on a transport. The ride was instruments all the way, nothing but sound and no movement, as traveling through sheer space in the register of absolute zero must be. Finally, they let down and landed at Tsuiki in southern Japan, just before noon. From there they took the train north.

It was an old car with worn plush upholstery on seats that released sudden puffs of dust when disturbed. Along the center of the ceiling ran a line of etched, opaque globes that cupped the bulbs; and all the fittings were yellow brass. Cleve settled back to watch through the water-rippled window the first hour or so of countryside. It was turning green beneath the wet, warming skies. The orange trees were dotted with fruit, cabbages were up, and the tea bushes gleaming. Only the rice stubble in the quilted, reflecting fields still appeared dormant. In the stations, vendors displayed slopes of candy, oranges, beer, and cigarettes on their stands.

He sat enjoying the gentle swaying of the car and a symphony of nostalgic sounds: the groaning of the axles, the subdued shriek of metal bindings, the iron clatter of the vestibules. They were traveling. They were fleeing, leaving the war behind. He had forgotten what it felt like to be going somewhere by train.

The satisfaction was as substantial as a liquid within him. He listened to the wheels pounding and watched the occasional flurries of clotted smoke that came back from the engine. He felt part of the country itself. There seemed nothing strange here, rather it was all very familiar and comfortable to him.

DeLeo opened his musette bag. He had a fifth of bourbon in it, and cans of shrimp and other food. They did not drink the bourbon. Instead, they bought Japanese beer in quart bottles at the stops, opened the shrimp and ate and talked. The afternoon went pleasantly that way, thinking back to other journeys and days, to what had happened and what was to come. DeLeo was a good companion. He had always traveled. He was at rest while moving, and less military than ever. They fell asleep before dark, leaning on their elbows on the window sills. The porter had to wake them up to make the berths.

Cleve stepped outside at one stop just before he went to bed. It was a damp night, but calm and clean-smelling. The country air nourished his whole body. He strolled down the concrete platform alongside the quiet, sleeping cars. After a while he reached the end of the overhead shed and, still further on, the head of the train. A stocky engine stood there in chaplets of steam and vapors. The signalman bowed politely toward him. Cleve remained for a few minutes of uncertainty, expecting to see the train budge to a start at any time. Then he walked back slowly. The sky above him was curdled gray.

In the morning they reached Atami and the eastern coast. The town was built in a valley and along the sides of the mountains, all overlooking the cold, blue water. Cleve watched it from his berth. He was reluctant to get up. He would have liked to finish the trip this way, luxuriously. For a long while he did stay like that, the pillow propped beneath his head. From Atami north, they skirted little fishing villages and followed a perilous, narrow strip of coastal road. Finally he got up. He washed lightly. Not more than thirty minutes later they were pulling into Tokyo.

They were rattling across the city, away from the station, in a taxi; and the tempo of everything had changed. The train had clattered through a night of leisure, but suddenly time began to race. It seemed to be streaming from them. There was an overwhelming sense of the vastness of the city. A year would have been inadequate for it. The few days they had to spend were dwarfed, and already every minute seemed to be one in which they were late for something.

The first hotel they tried had no rooms available. Neither had the second. They called the Club Heights and the Hosokawa. It was the same, filled up. They had not made reservations anywhere, and somehow, illogically, it seemed as if these hotels should be empty—they did not cater to Japanese, and almost everybody else ought to have been in Korea. DeLeo knew of others, however.

"Where?" Cleve wanted to know.

"The Astor is the nearest."

They drove there. It was a small, expensive hotel implanted on a hill and heavily walled like a castle or fortress. Despite this, there seemed to be something impermanent about it, as if it would not last any longer than the war did. A sign announced that the bar and restaurant were open twenty-four hours a day. The desk clerk bowed as they entered.

"Do you have any rooms?" DeLeo asked.

The clerk pushed a fountain-pen stand forward, without a word.

Their rooms were in front, with a commanding view of the neighborhood. They were neat though sparsely furnished; and a worn, flowered appearance made them seem very old. A humble odor that was nothing specific persisted in them even after the bellboy had opened the windows.

They left their bags and went down to the bar to have a drink in the gray, luminescent daylight. That early made it like being in a resort off-season. From the glass terrace they looked out across the low roofs of the city crowded beneath the sky. DeLeo called for a menu.

"What will it be for breakfast, Cleve?"

"I don't know. What do they have?"

"Everything. I think I'll order a steak."

"A steak. That sounds good. Order me one, too. And let's have another drink first, what do you say?"

"You're only old once," DeLeo grinned.

After eating, they went up to the rooms to bathe and go to bed. It was a good, free feeling to have had too many drinks before noon. Cleve decided to shower when he woke up. He took off his clothes and lay down on the soft, fresh-linened bed. He closed his eyes and felt sleep slowly come upon him, taking him down. He could hear faint hotel sounds through the floor and walls, and out in the streets the traffic, fainter still.

It was afternoon when they awoke. They took a taxi downtown. The city was enormous and teeming with life. Cleve could feel its vigor as they drove through it, down narrow streets, past the endless small, wooden houses with bedquilts hanging out over their upper windows to air and wash strung across their fronts. Schoolboys in simple black uniforms were strolling home in groups, and children in bright clothes, red mostly and sometimes plaid, ran past. A stream of bicyclists was always on both sides.

They stopped at the Gae-jo-en and went to the downstairs bar. DeLeo ordered martinis for them. It was still early, and the bar was empty. They were the only ones except for the bartender, polishing glasses. They finished two drinks apiece and went on to the Imperial. There, the first drinkers were just arriving, colonels of the staff, their ladies, and important-looking civilians. Cleve could feel the warmth of liquor spreading within him. As his eyes fell upon one person or another, he saw them with a clarity such that he would never forget what they looked like, and only seconds later as his glance moved on, he could not remember at all. He felt at once brilliant and doltish. He did not care. The only thing that bothered him was the grateful sense of well-being. It was good to be on firm land again, on earth, safe. His mortal knees had grown steady, but he was ashamed of it. He would have preferred not to have been so relieved and instead to have been uncomfortable, aching to return to combat.

He was not, though. He was happy, plungingly and briefly, like a runner who abandons a championship try halfway.

After a while, they walked outside into the mist. The blood was beating within them. Cleve gulped draughts of air. Down the wide, lighted boulevards and through the park they took a cab to the University Club. It was dark and reserved there. They went down a carpeted hallway, feeling the propriety of oak walls and the tall, carved doors. The cocktail lounge was livelier. A pianist was playing sentimental favorites. They sat at a table near this clear trickling of reminiscence that brought back forgotten years with each song.

"Another martini?" DeLeo said.

"Certainly. There's nothing like ten or fifteen before dinner."

"And we're here to enjoy civilization."

A waiter took their order, and DeLeo disappeared to make a telephone call. Cleve waited, looking around the room openly, in a mood that was between pleasure and intense longing. He saw two stunning Japanese girls enter with a group of Marine officers. The tables were thronged with couples. His nostrils took in the many perfumes.

Suddenly, not long after DeLeo had come back, it was too late to eat. It was past nine o'clock. The time had fled silently. Cleve lit a cigarette and watched its smoke as it was devoured. He felt himself racked by the sweetest of hungers. There was women's laughter in the room, and the sound of it overcame him with a flood of desire. He had suppressed it for months. Now it overflowed. He could hardly contain it, sitting there in the torment of desperate hunger. That was all there seemed to be of life now, the need to satisfy the hungers of the spirit and the flesh. Before, in what had amounted to a childhood extended, he had hardly been aware of them.

"I'm getting tired of this place, Bert," he said.

"Good. Let's leave."

"Where to?"

"Come on."

"I don't feel like drinking any more."

"I don't either. Come on. I made a call for us."

"Miyoshi's?" Cleve asked. He could hear his heart pumping within him.

"That's right."

They drove through the streets. Trains of lighted shops moved past. Trolley cars swayed in front of them, and bicyclists flashed among the traffic. They crossed a wide bridge and curved down a long grade, as if into another, more subdued plane of the city. A river gleamed black alongside the avenue. Cleve had lost track of where they were. He sat deep in the rear seat of the cab watching, as there streamed dizzily past the strange displays beyond which his thoughts had already gone. Everything was distorted except for the desire that held him completely, in a way only fear could match. Finally, they turned into an alleyway between plain shop-fronts and came into a dark courtyard. Someone came running out to open the door of the cab and lead them further. They reached an entrance flanked by garden stones. They changed their shoes to sandals and went in. There was muted music, floating along hallways floored with shining hardwood. They followed down these passages to a large, clean room, where they sat on tatami mats and waited. A girl brought kimonos for them. They took their uniforms off. She folded them neatly when she returned, stacked them on separate trays and took them out.

In the loose, laundered folds of the kimono, Cleve felt completely at peace. Even the vestments of the war were gone. He nibbled at what must have been fish pretzels on a tray. Soon the door slid open again, and two elaborately costumed, scrubbed girls entered, bowing politely, and sat down between them. They seemed as demure as schoolgirls. They talked shyly in broken English, giving their names. After a while, one went for a samisen. They reclined and listened to her play and sing in a distorted, high, haunting voice. The girls sat respectfully upright. One of the songs was "China Night." It was DeLeo's favorite. *Shina no yoru.* They played it again and again for him, one singing and the other humming. A serving girl brought warm vials of wine on a tray.

Later, they went to the baths. They sang while the girls washed and rinsed them, and then climbed down together, all of them, into the smooth sand-colored tile pool. The water was clear and scalding. Everything was washed away. He floated in a dream of disconnected languor. The girl was in it, too, with her flawless skin and sturdy body sensuously distorted beneath the surface. Her hair was done up carefully, piled on her head, protected by a towering towel. She had abandoned the virtuous reserve of upstairs. She caressed him beneath the water. She presented herself to him deliberately. They laughed at nothing. They played like children in the steamy room.

In the thick bedroll on the tatami floor, she was as obliging as a new wife. He woke up twice during the night. She was instantly awake and seemingly pleased both times.

The next morning they were in the baths again at seven o'clock, sitting naked on the wooden stools or in the hot water, shaving. The soaking was like being born again. Outside, through the windows, the morning looked gray, and Cleve noticed a light scum on the surface of the fish ponds, but the spell was not gone. He was still king. He and DeLeo were brothers, sharing the riches of empire together. Beyond the roofs, he could see the tips of distant smokestacks with their blackened mouths beginning to issue smoke as the working day started for lesser men.

"We should never come back here, Bert," he said. They were on a plateau of existence somehow, between safety and doom.

"Why not?"

"This is the greatest life in the world."

"Certain parts."

"All of it. It's the way to die, too."

"I keep thinking there must be a better way," DeLeo said.

"No. The way to go is in an instant, reaching for that highest one of the stars and then falling away, disappearing, against the earth. I wouldn't mind that, would you?"

"Some of your ideas, Cleve . . ."

"Ridiculous, eh? I've carried them around for years; and now, at the time they ought to be the truest, so few of them are worth a damn.

"Odd. Everything about this ought to be perfect for you and me. Here we are, by sheer accident, in the most natural of worlds, and of course that means the most artificial, because we're very civilized. We're in a child's dream and a man's heaven, living a medieval life under sanitary conditions, flying the last shreds of something irreplaceable, I don't know what, in a sport too kingly even for kings. Nothing is missing, and yet it's the men who don't understand it at all that become its heroes."

DeLeo listened quietly.

"Or maybe they do understand," Cleve said, "and I don't. Tell me, Bert, what do you think is important here?"

"It's a war," DeLeo said. "MIGs."

"Nothing else?"

"Staying alive."

"That's not very much."

"Without the MIGs, the rest doesn't matter."

"You may be right."

"Believe me."

"My God, though, if someone tries . . ."

"It's not enough. In this greatest life of yours, you have to win."

Cleve was silent for a while. He lathered his face and began to shave.

"If it's not enough," he repeated, "this isn't anything to be proud of."

"Maybe it's enough for me. Not for you, though."

"We're the same."

"Not really," DeLeo said.

Cleve glanced briefly at him lolling in the bath, the water up to his neck and his eyes closed. When he looked back in the mirror, everything had changed somehow. The passionate moments had passed. It was as if the harsh light of day had suddenly fallen full on them.

The girls attended them until they were dressed and ready to leave. They seemed to share a regret that it was over with.

"You rear gentreman," Cleve's said to him hesitantly.

"We're no gentlemen."

"Yes, yes, you are."

"No."

She smiled. She seemed very small now and young.

"You good captain," she insisted.

"No."

"No good captain?"

DeLeo laughed.

"She knows you, all right," he said. "No-good captain."

She was such a child. Cleve felt like a fool standing there. "Goodbye," he said.

"Yes. Guddo-bai." Then quietly, "Guddo-bai."

14

They did not stay long at the Astor. That morning, DeLeo began packing. He had made some telephone calls and arranged for them to move to the Hosokawa. Cleve was not enthusiastic.

"Why?" he asked. "This place seems fine to me."

"You'll like it better there. I guarantee it."

"I don't like moving. Does it have a bar?"

"Of course."

"A barber shop?"

"No barber shop."

"I knew it," Cleve said. "We'll have to shave ourselves there."

"What an inconvenience. Why don't you get started packing?"

"It's just that I'm accustomed to service. And this fellow here is a terrific barber."

"How do you know? You shaved yourself this morning."

"I like the way he limps."

"I haven't noticed him doing any limping."

"He has a bad leg. I think he was wounded in the war. I've been looking forward to hearing about it tomorrow morning with a nice hot towel on my face."

"Come on. Maybe we can come back some time for a haircut."

It was not a long trip. The Hosokawa was less than half a mile away. Despite himself, Cleve liked it the moment he entered. It had once been the residence of a prince, and beautifully maintained grounds encircled it. Also, it was distinctly more Oriental. They had to remove their shoes at the entrance and put on the hotel's slippers.

They stopped at the bar for a drink and read through the newspapers. There was not much in them about the war. The front was quiet, and there had been no air action at all. They went in to lunch. The dining room opened onto the gardens. It was a rare afternoon. Sunshine made the evergreens glisten, and a stream as clear as ice passed soundlessly among carefully set rocks streaked with pale moss. They were the only ones eating. There was, overall, the dignity of a great estate. The food was excellent. They had not had breakfast and were hungry.

That night they started at the Mimatsu, which DeLeo called a place of great historical interest. For reasons of his own, he said. It was a night club the size of an auditorium. Hostesses in evening gowns came to sit with them.

"Fighter pirot, no?" one said, smiling.

"How can you tell?"

"Aw same fighter pirot, big here," she pointed to her wrist where a watch might be, then to her lap, "sma' here."

To applaud the floor show they were given a kind of fireworks that exploded into confetti. Each act was followed by a barrage of sharp explosions and blizzards of colored paper drifting through the spotlight beams. DeLeo's girl wore a dress of tight, violet satin. She said that her name was Sunday. She looked more Indonesian than Japanese and had dazzling, even teeth.

"Every day is a horiday with me," she smiled.

It was like a musical comedy about shore leave, Cleve thought. There was a fountain bathed in rainbow lighting in the center of the dance floor. DeLeo was drinking and breaking the glasses. People at other tables turned around every time he smashed one, shouting, and the waiter charged him for a glass each round. The olives from martinis were lined up in soldierly rows on the tablecloth. There were twenty-five olives in a martini squadron, he explained.

"Sleep is a bad habit you get into as a baby," he said, and they went on to the Bacchus.

The floor show there was unvarying, strip teases on a small dance floor closely surrounded by tables, and the girls took everything off but their high-heeled shoes. The last one stripped at the beginning of her act and danced naked to a tango for five minutes, pausing to sit on laps and drink from glasses held eagerly to her as she did. DeLeo was introducing Cleve as Professor Pell, the father of the famous flier.

"Can't we get away from him for a few days?" Cleve said.

"Friendo!" a voice interrupted loudly. It was a second lieutenant with a face as flat as the sole of a shoe, leaning across the table. He was drunk. "Did I hear right? Are you in that fabulous Pell's squadron?"

"It's not exactly his squadron yet," Cleve said.

The lieutenant threw back his head and laughed.

"Ha, ha," he said. "It may be soon if I know the Doctor. How is he doing? I hear he has two MIGs already."

"Yes."

"That old son of a bitch. You know, I'm probably the best friend he has. I've known him for years."

"Lucky you," DeLeo said.

The lieutenant was heedless.

"He really is an old son of a bitch. Watch out for him. Especially at cards. He's a terror."

Cleve took a last swallow from his drink.

"Are you ready to go, Bert?" he asked.

"No, not yet."

"So you're in the same squadron with the Doctor," the lieutenant said. "Goddamn me. Did I tell you about when we were in flying school together? He was cadet captain. You probably can't believe that, knowing Pell, but it's a fact. I don't know how he did it. He was always in some mess, but damn me if they didn't make him cadet captain.

"One time we were in the barracks, and he was looking out the window and saw this puss coming down the street. Man, you should have seen her. Built, you know what I mean. He gives a big whistle. Shake it, honey, he says, but don't break it. She just turned around and gave him this hard look. Well, damn if it didn't turn out to be the commandant's wife. I mean it. The Doctor thought he'd had it, but she didn't get a good enough look at him. They came around to the barracks five minutes later to find out who it was. Lined everybody up. The colonel, himself, and he was really mad, but Pell just looked him right in the eye. He was in some trouble like that all the time, but lucky, you know. He'd lie out of it some way, that son of a bitch. He's really fabulous. He got to be cadet captain. Imagine that. I laughed myself sick. The Doctor. He really had them snowed."

"Let's go," Cleve said, standing up.

"He's a terrific guy, though. The best. You just have to get to know him."

As they left, the lieutenant was telling them to give his regards to Pell, that son of a bitch, he said. They drove back to the hotel in a cab, through the riotous night of the city.

"Well, friendo," DeLeo said, "how does it feel in Pell's squadron?"

"You sound happy."

"I am."

"Well, don't be so happy," Cleve said. "I knew it all along. I knew it before you did."

"You sure hid it then."

"Yes."

"Why the hell didn't you do something? Why didn't you get rid of him?"

"I don't know," Cleve replied. "It's too late now, anyway. It's gone too far, and I let it. You can't just turn that over to somebody else."

"Why not? That's what I want to know."

"It's mine to finish," Cleve said.

They stopped at the bar for one last drink before going to their rooms. The bar girl appeared noiselessly. She was pretty, with a bright complexion. Her smile seemed something from earlier, sunny hours.

"Two Scotches with a little water," Cleve said.

She brought the drinks and turned the record player on. It was a type that took only one disc at a time, and she stood beside it and put records on for them, one by one. Soft, unidentifiable music filled the room.

While they sat there drinking in silence, a tall, exotic-looking girl came in. She was wearing the cotton wraparound that the hotel supplied for going to the baths, and slippers. She sat down. After a while, she started a listless conversation with the bar girl, in Japanese. Her head was down as she talked, and she looked at nothing but the polished wood surface of the bar. Suddenly she began to cry. It did not appear to be in reaction to anything that had been said, and as she sobbed, Cleve felt discomfort. It seemed he was obliged to say something.

"Don't cry," he said a little awkwardly. "What's wrong?"

She did not lift her gaze.

"Can I be any help?"

She shook her head.

"What's the trouble?"

"Nothing."

"Tell me."

"No."

There was a long, awkward silence. Cleve did not make a further advance. He sat watching her.

"My man is going," she said at last. "He's leaving Japan. He's taking the train tomorrow morning early, to sail for the States."

Cleve did not say anything.

"This is the last night we're together. It's not easy to know that. It's not easy to say goodbye."

"I guess not."

"He is going to try to come back right away," she said. "He thinks he can do it. There is some way he thinks he can arrange it. He says that, but he won't be back. I know. After tomorrow morning, I don't see him again."

"Maybe you will. How long has he been stationed here?"

"Three years. Three years, and I've known him almost since the beginning, when he first came. Now he's leaving. Do you know what that's like?"

"I suppose so."

She did not say anything for perhaps a full minute.

"How will it be when he's gone?" she said. "I think of that. I don't know what to do. I don't have anywhere to go."

"Haven't you got a home?"

"Home!" she laughed thinly.

"Don't you have one?"

"Home? Yes, I have one. Do you know what it's like? It's an icebox. My mother and father wouldn't speak to me. What would I do there? There's nobody that cares anything about me now."

"Don't you have any brothers or sisters?"

"No. Not now."

"Not even a dog?" Cleve asked. He meant it as a joke.

"I'll never go back," she said.

Cleve did not answer.

"I think I'll go down south to one of the air bases and get a job there. Do you know anything about that?" She was suddenly interested and intense. "They have a lot of jobs at the airfields, don't they?"

"I guess so. It depends on what kind of a job you want."

"I think I'll be a secretary. They make a good salary."

"Can you type?"

"No."

"You probably won't get a job as a secretary then."

"Oh, no? Well, I will." She was proud. "What do they expect me to do? Be a maid and scrub floors? I've been married almost for three years."

She did not say much after that. She began combing her hair. She asked for a glass of water. A few minutes later, a big, handsome young man came in, also in slippers and a robe which was too small for him. Its sleeves hit between his elbow and wrist. He sat down beside her. They talked quietly to each other, head to head. Cleve had become an intruder. They danced briefly to the music and then moved across the room to sit together on one of the couches. She leaned her head on his shoulder. The bar girl—he called her Mary—brought them drinks, but they left without touching them. There was only the music then, filling the empty room.

"She can't go to her home," Mary said, "because he's an American."

"Is that bad?" Cleve asked.

"Japanese boys won't have her now."

It seemed very quiet in the bar.

"How about you, Mary?" DeLeo asked.

"Yes?"

"Don't you have a boyfriend?"

She surrendered a shy smile but did not answer.

"Well, do you?"

"Yes."

"Where is he?"

"Not here."

"Not in Tokyo?"

"He isn't here."

"I understand that all right. Where is he, though?"

She seemed embarrassed. She walked the length of the bar to place another record on the machine.

"He's not here yet," she said.

"Not yet?"

"No. Same as brue bud."

"What?"

"Brue bud."

"What did she say, Cleve?"

"I didn't understand it, either. The what, Mary?"

"The brue bud. Of happiness," she added.

"Oh, the bluebird," DeLeo said.

"Yes," she smiled. "To come here some day."

"I guess so."

Cleve went to bed feeling very tired. He could hear the chirping of insects outside, and the continuous, high call of crickets. He lay quietly, looking into the darkness with unblinking eyes. He was thinking of the girl who would not be a maid and the other who waited for her American lover. He envied them. He would have liked to enter their fairy tale with them, their opera; for it seemed somehow that, despite the sadness, when the curtain fell they would find the youth in them to laugh and go elsewhere. But he had stepped into an arena. He had joined a dark, ultimate battle, as all the while the current of days bore him slowly down.

15

The morning was blue with a warm wind blowing. They ate a late breakfast, and when Cleve took out his wallet afterward, he came upon something he had almost forgotten, a note of introduction to a Mr. Miyata whose brother had been a friend of Cleve's father in Washington, before the war. Cleve smoothed the folded piece of paper. He had been given it in the States, in the event he had the occasion to be in Tokyo. He looked at the address again and tried to imagine where it might be. Through the city on a fine day to see something of its lesser parts, he considered that for a while. In the afternoon, not knowing what to expect, he went to call.

Miyata was an artist, known to a degree as a leader of the young antitraditionalists. The studio where he lived and worked was in an outlying section. Cleve's driver had trouble finding it. The address was straightforward; but in the provincial suburbs, even the police could not direct them to it. Finally, a grocer in the neighborhood was able to point out the right street. It was narrow and climbed a steep hill. They labored up it, pausing to search for house numbers. At last they stopped before the right one. There, set back at the end of a concrete path and in the midst of untended lawn, stood a small, weathered house. As he crossed the patio on which a trio of glass doors opened, Cleve caught a glimpse of someone standing inside. He knocked at the door. It was opened after a pause. Cleve introduced himself and presented the note. The man he assumed was Miyata read it quickly, breathed an audible assent, smiled, looked up, and offered his hand, apparently pleased to receive the visitor. He confirmed the relationship so readily this way that Cleve had an uneasy feeling he had never really heard of anyone named Connell.

"Come in, sir," Miyata said.

He was a gray-haired man in his late forties. He seemed much younger. Small, but firm-skinned and muscular, everything about him implied great energy.

Cleve was invited to remove his shoes in a narrow, sunken entrance just inside the door and follow into the house. The exterior had been deceiving. They came into a large, well-lit room that seemed to be more than the house could have contained. In one corner were piles of books. Everywhere else were canvases. They were stacked against the walls. They hung side by side, higher up. Cleve stood in the center of the room and stared. The work of years was here in a style muted but commanding. He had never seen anything like them. The colors were dominated by blue and gray with Oriental mood and pose. Many were nudes, some life size. The eye slid from their frankness, but still they were so religious, with such patient, calm devotion, that Cleve felt himself held undisturbedly before them.

There was a couch, a few chairs, and a coffee table. Everything else was working materials. Curled tubes of paint littered the floor like lead grubs. It was a spring afternoon. They drank lemon soda and talked. As they did, Cleve felt he had somehow entered a level of the city that he had not imagined existed.

Miyata was fluent and intelligent. Nothing was beyond his curiosity. He seemed to be above the confusion of life, as if he had been commissioned to spend his own in undisturbed judgment of the world about him, protected always by a mandate from the gods. They spoke briefly of Korea and then of the past war with the United States. Miyata had been in Japan for its entire duration and must have been deeply affected, but when he talked about it, it was without bitterness. Wars were not of his doing. He considered them almost poetically, as if they were seasons, the cruel winters of man, even though almost all of the work he had done in the 1930s and early 1940s had been lost when his house was burned in the great incendiary raid of 1944. He described the night vividly, the endless hours, the bombers thundering low over the storms of fire.

"All of your work?" Cleve said. "It must have been like being killed yourself."

Miyata smiled.

"One would think so," he replied, "and I, myself, did at first, but no, it was not. It was finally like being born again, I decided. I started life for a second time."

They talked of Japan, of France where he had lived and studied for six years, of Tahiti, and the former Japanese-mandated islands in the Pacific. His opinions and observations were all somehow fresh. They seemed not to be preconceived, but as if he were bringing them forth for the first time. They talked about the movies. Miyata was very interested in them. He knew and had seen all the great ones, American, French, Russian, Italian—anything that had played in Japan.

"It must be the most difficult of the arts," he said, "combining all the others; and for it to be perfect, every part of it must be."

They wandered over to the part of the room where the books

were strewn. There were Japanese movie magazines and five or six bound annuals, along with definitive volumes on films and their history. They leafed through these, sometimes pausing to discuss specific pictures they had both seen. Cleve found it strange. It was an unexpected interest for a man like Miyata to have. It was all hard to believe. Somehow, idly, he had made his way here, to this small house above the city, far from any of the world he knew. It was a strange reality in which he was not sure of anything, only the pleasure of a few uncommon hours. He stared out the broad windows. They had talked for a long time.

In the late afternoon he heard someone at the entrance, setting shoes down in the well there. He glanced over his shoulder. It was a girl. When she saw that there was a visitor, she turned not to enter the room, but Miyata called her in. She came forward a few steps. As he saw her clearly for the first time, Cleve felt the moment would be one of the few remaining to the end.

"This is my daughter, Eiko."

"How do you do," Cleve said, hearing his own voice isolated and distinct. It sounded absurd.

She dropped her gaze.

"How do you do, sir," she said. It was polite and disinterested.

Her hair was perfectly black and as fine as a young child's. She was nineteen. She stood in the splendor of that, calm and confident beyond words. She was on the walls of the studio, too, he was certain. It was an effort not to look and see her in the paintings.

16

The next day was Sunday. He spent the early afternoon at Miyata's. He had brought two cartons of American cigarettes with him as a gift, and around the table, on which was a bowl of fruit as voluptuous as colored photographs, they sat, drinking tea and smoking. Eiko sat with them. She took little part in the conversation, but her silence seemed merely polite. Cleve felt certain that her thoughts were full of things she could have said but did not. He could hardly keep his eyes from her. Every glance made him need another.

Later, he rode with her, bicycling through oddly connected streets, down hills, and past unexpected stretches of green park. They walked the bicycles up a final steep grade and turned off the street between a whitewashed lane of trees, at the end of which a small lake was hidden. They sat in a shaded spot on the shore. Opposite them, across the still, reflecting surface was a bank of heavy, sloping masonry, soaked with moss. It was like the wall of a moat. Close beyond it ran a defiladed road. They saw the heads of occasional strollers. Nothing else was in motion, except four ducks that searched the shallow water nearby for food, in a single file, as if drilling.

He had almost forgotten how to enjoy such an hour, how to stop counting days, missions, kills. He breathed deeply. The afternoon was warm. There was a dreamlike air of isolation. He sat with her happily, letting the world move on without him. Their talk was filled with long, unanxious pauses. Quietly they spoke to each other, as if waiting meanwhile for the shy inner person to emerge.

At first he thought that he was learning something of Japan as it really was, but slowly he began to doubt that. She was her father's daughter, not entirely Japanese. She was somewhere between Japan and the West, unique, just as the remote, soft-singing islands in the Pacific were between.

He felt himself drawn gently forth. She had that gift of silence that surpasses speech, the elusiveness that allows itself to be endowed. He smiled when she confessed to wanting to be an actress. It was so unthinkable. She seemed so completely fine and unequipped. She was determined, though, even to an exact ambition. It was modest, as perhaps a constellation seems modest: to be in a single great film, only that; to be part of something that people all over the world would acclaim, and in which through the years she would always be the same.

"You want to be a goddess forever," Cleve said.

She felt for the answer in the grass beneath her fingertips and spoke to it.

"That would be perfect."

"Of course."

There was a long pause. They lay in the cool grass, side by side, unwilling to do anything that might change it.

"What is your ambition?" she asked after a while.

Cleve closed his eyes. There had been many ambitions, all of them true at the time. They were scattered behind him like the ashes of old campfires, though he had warmed himself at every one of them. Now an ambition had been forced upon him, but he hesitated. The innocence of a girl could have no values by which to judge him. What is your ambition?

"It's hard to trace," he said. "It was simple at first. When I was a boy, I wanted to be like my father. He's retired now, but he was in the navy. A captain."

His eyes were closed. He was trying to pare away the complications of a lifetime.

"For a long time I never even bothered to consider anything else. I was going to the naval academy, like he did. It was understood. My brothers could do anything they chose, but I was the oldest. I had a responsibility."

"You went?"

"Oh, yes. Not for very long. You took a physical the day you arrived, and I didn't pass. It seems funny now, but it was very serious. There were a lot of jokes during the war about old women on streetcars saying, 'What is a fine, healthy young man like you doing out of uniform?' None of them ever asked me, but I was ready. 'Madam,' I was going to say, 'I have albumin in my urine.' "

"I don't understand," she said.

"It's not important. It's only important not to have it if you're going to be a naval officer. My youngest brother finally went to Annapolis, so that made up for it in a way. By then I was grateful. It sort of left me to myself a little."

"How many brothers are you?"

"Three," Cleve replied. "An unusual family. Not one of us fought in the war. Not even my father. He commanded things, of course, a cruiser once, but never where there was fighting. That's really why he retired. He was sure he'd never overcome the disadvantages of that. It was worse for me, though. I joined the Air Force when the war was almost over. I went 'overseas' just as everybody else was coming back. Not even to a place where there had been war, at that. To Panama. Do you know where that is?"

"Yes. The canal."

"That's right."

He could hear the ducks. He opened his eyes to glance at them, white as handkerchiefs against the water's edge.

"It was Panama," he said softly. "You know what fighters are? The airplanes?"

She nodded.

"I really started flying them there."

"Dangerous, neh?" she said. "My father says it takes bravery."

"In a way," Cleve answered. "I can't explain it. At first it's dangerous. Then it changes. It's a sport. You belong to it. More than that. Finally it becomes, I don't know, a refuge. The sky is the godlike place. If you fly it alone, it can be everything."

He stopped talking and then found he wanted to go on.

"One Sunday, like this, it was in the early summer, there was Korea. I couldn't wait to go. I thought I knew what I was supposed to do."

"What is that?"

"The point is," he said, "you do a thing well. You devote yourself to it, and after a while pride arrives, plain, fatal pride. You're happy in yourself, at last. You do something well, like your wanting to be in one good picture, one really fine one.

"Well, here is the place where the fighter pilots live, and if you shoot down five planes you join a group, a core of heroes. Nothing less can do it."

"You've done that?"

"Oh, no. I've shot down one."

"A man like yourself, perhaps," she said.

"I hope so. I hope it was no frightened boy. I want this to be the end, anyway. And when you make your last appearance, before whatever audience you have, you want it to be your real performance, to say, somehow, remember me for this. I've never said that to anyone.

"You know, truth doesn't always come from truthful men. I have this colonel, wing commander, who would never stand in awe of truth; but he said it one day, one miserable morning: 'There are a few men who go beyond the rest.' If it's fallen to you to do that, there's no other way. You ask for my ambition: it's that. Not to fail."

"And afterward?"

He opened his hands.

"But what will you do?" she asked. "What do you want to do?"

He did not answer.

In the spring afternoon they lay, the light falling on them. There was no future or past. There was the slow, immortal beating of his blood, somehow in time with hers he wanted to imagine.

"We must go," she said at last.

"Not yet."

"Please. It's late."

He sat up.

"Will I see you tomorrow?"

"I hope."

Another day. Cleve began to try to plan it. He wanted to be able to present it to her, perfect, like a gift.

They stood for a minute before they left, leaning on the bicycles and watching the ducks. He thought, as the day faded and they made their way back through the dusk, of what he had not said. To come back. To stay in Japan. It was not impossible. He suddenly felt the light-headedness of thinking that he had not passed the time of choices. He left Miyata's reluctantly and drove by taxi through a city he was beginning to feel he knew. He arrived at the Hosokawa as soft as a man waking from sleep.

DeLeo was in the bar with Guthrie, a pilot from one of the other squadrons. Cleve sat down with them. It was dark outside by then, and the room's dim lights created a texture of hotel velvet, although all the upholstery was cotton.

"You just get in?" Cleve asked Guthrie.

"This morning."

"How are things back at Kimpo?"

"Haven't you heard?"

"What?"

"Where have you been all day?" DeLeo asked.

"Bicycling around town."

"Bicycling. Well, that's living, I suppose. Have a drink."

Cleve ordered one. The bar girl, her mouth hiding its smile, brought it.

"Thank you. You're a lovely girl, Mary, do you know?"

The smile broke out.

"Well, Bert," he said, "here's to your children."

"Whoever they are. Have you really been riding a bicycle all day?"

"Absolutely. Most of the day, anyway."

"You have, eh? Have you heard the news?"

"No. Is the war over? Nothing would make me happier right now."

"There was a big fight yesterday afternoon. We lost three ships."

Cleve's stomach went empty as if under a blow. There had been a big fight, and he had been in Tokyo. He felt like a man washed overboard a thousand miles from shore.

"Who?" he asked.

"Desmond in your squadron for one," Guthrie said.

"Desmond? How did it happen?"

"He got hit and had to bail out. They saw his chute open."

"Where was it?"

"Right on the river."

Up at the Yalu. It seemed a planet away. Desmond was alone up there, on the green bottom of the great sea of air in the most crushing solitude. In one agonizing moment of departure he had fallen from loftiness to doom, to the hostile earth where he became trembling prey.

"Did they get any MIGs?" Cleve asked.

"Eight."

It was even worse than he had thought. He felt his mouth weaken.

"There must have been a lot of them up," he said.

"More than I've ever seen, but that's not all."

"Christ, what more? Pell make ace?"

"No, nothing like that," Guthrie said.

"What?"

"Casey Jones is back."

Cleve could suddenly hear his own heart and beyond it a faded Guthrie talking about markings, the black stripes. The words were indistinct. He was back. He had come back, like a lost planet, a dark star, changing the whole firmament. There was nothing but that, like a cry of plague. Cleve stared at his watch. Guthrie was still talking.

"I'm going up to pack."

"Pack?" DeLeo said.

"There's a plane we can go back on tonight."

"We've got two days left," DeLeo protested.

"And we'll be there in the morning."

"For Christ's sake," DeLeo complained, "what's the hurry? Use your head. We won't get another leave for months. I've got a regular volcano lined up at the Bacchus tonight."

"Guthrie can take care of her."

"The hell he can."

"I don't care," Cleve said. "Stay if you want to. I'm going back."

"Goddamn it," DeLeo began, but he was already alone. He finished his drink in a swallow and followed.

"Get one for me," he heard Guthrie call from the bar.

There was no way to telephone her. In his room, Cleve sat down and hurriedly wrote a note.

. . . I'd hoped to see you tomorrow, but I've just learned that I must go back to my squadron tonight. The war.

I don't know when I'll be able to come to Tokyo again, in two months, perhaps. It seems a long time. Summer. All the talking we did, all the things unsaid, at least that I meant to say. Next time.

As they left the hotel, he gave the addressed envelope to a cab driver to deliver.

Riding out to the airfield, he watched the lights of the city grow thinner as they passed to its shallows and beyond. It seemed, somehow, that the leave had vanished in a few crowded hours.

17

They landed at Seoul at 5:30 in the morning. It was chilly, with mist lying gray in the land hollows. The wind blew fitfully and shifted a fine dust across the ground. The flight had been miserable. Imprisoned in the cold, sepulchral cabin of the transport, they had sat for almost five hours listening to the clamor of the engines and the chorus of shrill rattles that continually traveled the whole length of the ship in resonant phases. A pale dawn had at last appeared outside the windows and ended their sleeplessness, although it was some time before the strewn, crowded interior became light. There was the hush of early day over the countryside when they drove on to Kimpo, shivering a little and feeling a metallic emptiness in their bellies.

In the mess, everything seemed the same. There were a few tables of sleepy men, up for the early mission, eating breakfast in a silence broken only by the ring of utensils. Cleve had two pancakes, as thick as his thumb, with butter and thin tart syrup, and drank three cups of the canned orange juice, cold and tongue-puckering. He asked around about the day's missions. There were four scheduled. The second one was to brief at 1015. They walked down the road to the barracks. It was still before seven. Everyone in the room was asleep. He lay on his cot for a long while before he was able to summon up his weariness to possess him.

The sound of ships returning from a mission awakened him. He listened in semi-awareness to them passing overhead and then looked at his watch. 0915. He sat up, his face near the window. Some more were coming. Their sound preceded them slightly. He saw them go by, moving like thrown spears, two of them, without tanks. After a minute came two more. He left the window and stood up, feeling drugged. The water on his face, as he shaved, revived him somewhat. He noticed DeLeo beginning to stir. It was soon 0930. In a few minutes they would have to start down for the briefing. While he was waiting for DeLeo to get dressed, Daughters came in.

"I wanted to make sure you were up. I thought you might want to go on this next one," he explained.

"Have the names been posted yet?"

"Nolan's waiting for you to give him ours."

"Nolan. Is he taking Desmond's place?" He tried to sound matter-of-fact.

"I guess so," Daughters said.

"I see." He did not, though. There was an unwanted silence.

"We didn't expect you back so soon," Daughters said. "Was Tokyo closed?"

"We were having too good a time," DeLeo muttered.

"We had a bad one here. I suppose you heard."

"We heard all right," DeLeo said. "Has there been any word on Desmond?"

"No, nothing."

As they waited outside for a ride, Cleve noticed three small locust trees between the barracks that were turning green. They stood huddled together on an embankment like three lost children. Suddenly he realized that it was relatively mild out. The winter had gone at last. The air was alive. It felt good to breathe it. Walking into combat operations, he saw that a fringe of palest grass was growing in the seams of the rotted sandbag barricades.

Pell was waiting for them inside.

"Hey, welcome home," he said. "Thought you were safe in Tokyo."

"Don't be wise."

"You sound mean, Captain. Well, you might see some action today."

"What happened on the last mission?"

"They sighted a lot of MIGs, that's all," Pell replied. "No fight."

They went in to the briefing room and sat down. In the row behind him, Cleve heard someone talking about the black-striped MIG.

"Diagonal. Five diagonal markings."

"Five? How do you know it's five?"

"Ask anybody. Ask Intelligence if you don't believe me."

"Have you seen him?"

"Yes, I've seen him."

"You and the colonel, eh?"

"It was from a distance, but I tell you I saw him."

The word had spread through the group like a stain. Everybody was looking for Casey Jones, secretly, guarding their motives. Whether they sought to fight or avoid him, they were full of restless expectation. He was being seen everywhere, sometimes simultaneously.

The briefing began. Cleve listened mechanically. Only the weather seemed to make an impression on him. It was forecast to be fair all through the area with visibility unrestricted. The sun would be high during the period they were north. The weather officer gave its azimuth and elevation in degrees. Cleve felt like a patient listening to a description of an operation he was going to undergo.

Imil stepped onto the stage.

"They'll be up this time," he said, "so watch out. Don't take any chances, especially with that striped one. He may look alone, but he never is, and if you want to get back, keep your eyes open. Look high. That's where the ones you don't see until it's too late come from. That's it. Remember you're fighter pilots. Let's fight!"

After the briefing, Cleve lay down on one of the benches in the locker room and tried to sleep a little. There was more than an hour before start-engines time, and he was still tired. It was difficult to even doze, however. The hard bench denied any comfortable position. Sluggish flies buzzed about and found any bare skin. He was constantly brushing them off his hands, face, and ankles. He spent half an hour that way, dropping off to sleep sometimes but never relaxing. At the end he felt irritable and less rested.

He stood up and started to dress slowly. The room was filling up. There was talking and slamming of locker doors. Pell was assuring Hunter that the MIGs would be up this time, too.

"We'll catch them crossing at the reservoir," he said. "That's where they've been coming over."

He turned to Cleve.

"We ought to stay close to the reservoir," he advised, "and high."

"I'll decide where we go."

"Only trying to help you out," Pell smiled.

"When I need help, I'll ask for it."

Pell shrugged.

"If you don't want to be where the MIGs are . . ." he began.

"We'll be where they are."

"We'd better stay close to the reservoir, then."

"Oh, shut up, Pell," DeLeo said. "You don't know as much about it as you think."

"How many MIGs have you got?" Pell asked.

DeLeo reddened. "Don't brag on your luck," he said angrily.

"Luck? There's no luck involved."

"Don't talk so much, Pell," Cleve interrupted.

"Say, what's going on here anyway? What's the problem?"

"You're boring everybody."

"Too bad. We'll see who gets the MIGs, eh?"

The room had grown quiet. Everybody was listening. It was a moment Cleve and even all of them had been expecting.

"That's right, Pell," he said. "We'll see."

He turned and continued putting on his equipment. It seemed unusually heavy and restrictive. The dinghy felt like a loaded suitcase. He picked it up, then his parachute, and walked out toward his ship. His feet scuffed at the ground. He inspected his airplane. As he moved around it, he looked up several times at the sky. The first fair-weather cumulus was there, like spring flowers showing in the fields. He felt as if under the influence of a strong stimulant. He wanted to move his hands, to let his body take the tempo, absorb the energy that was inside him. Even after he had climbed into the cockpit and strapped himself down, he sat uncomfortably, thinking of what had been said, honing himself. His fingers ran blindly over the switches. His feet tapped the rudder pedals.

On takeoff, he noticed for the first time that the rice paddies surrounding Kimpo were turning green. He watched the ground flowing beneath him. There was one small farm that had three tall poplars in front of the house, giving it shade. They swept across it. Now, in motion, he felt somewhat better. They picked up speed and began to climb. He was aware of an elusive, mystic sensation supporting the physical as they went up.

It was a beautiful day. The coarse, brown peninsula looked peaceful. The snow had vanished from the mountains, and the rivers were free of ice. The sea was like an immense piece of jade through his sunglasses. Along the many crestlines were veins that gleamed like silver when the sun hit them. Thick green crowns were beginning to appear, and even the clay and sand seemed brighter. Low, scattered puffs of clouds looked like foam flecks on an even surf.

Just past Sinanju, there was a call: dust was rising from the runway at Antung. A rush of uneasiness came over him. His forearms and shoulders felt loose. There was a high, inaudible tone in the air, the thin skewer of fear. Every sensation was as if it had never happened to him before. The sky seemed plagued with invisible dangers.

As he reached the Yalu near Antung, he heard a flight dropping tanks for six ships passing above them at thirty-six thousand feet. They were all heading down the river. He looked up toward the reservoir, but saw nothing. He started a turn in that direction.

"Two o'clock high, Black," DeLeo called.

He had spotted them at the same instant, four of them out to the south at a higher altitude. He turned toward them to put them at twelve o'clock. They were headed in his direction. He could not identify them yet. He watched them intensely, as the slow seconds brought them together.

"They're MIGs," he heard Pell say.

Suddenly they were close, and there was no longer any doubt. Cleve felt an awesome disbelief as they passed above him, and he saw the detached-looking tails, like those on the celluloid birds that twirled at circuses.

"Drop tanks," he said.

The empty containers fell away, leaving his ship light and fast. It was like kicking off a pair of shoes in the water. The turn to follow the MIGs as they passed had put DeLeo and Hunter closer to them than Cleve, but still not close enough it appeared. There would be a long, useless chase. Just as Cleve was assessing it, he suddenly saw two more MIGs off to his right that would be crossing overhead in a moment as evenly as if it were all happening at an intersection. He called them out and began turning immediately to come out parallel to or behind them. Too high, he thought quickly. They were just a little too high.

There was not much time to decide. He started pulling his nose up sharply to get a snap shot perhaps, as they went by above him. If he was lucky, he might damage one and slow it down. It was all an act of balance. He had his nose high enough, but his speed was falling off rapidly. He would be slow and vulnerable.

"Am I clear?"

No response. He glanced about. Nothing. At the last second he could hold that steep pitch, the trailing MIG moved into his gunsight. He squeezed. The tracers floated out. His heart burgeoned. Part of his burst was hitting near the tail. A thin line of smoke began to follow the MIG.

He dropped his nose. As it came down heavily, he completed

his turn. He was not too far behind, about ten thousand feet, and two or three thousand feet below. He watched the MIG intently. Smoke was still coming from it, and then he saw that it was dropping behind the leader. He had crippled it. He could feel himself gaining, although he was unable to actually detect it yet. Then he heard Pell.

"I can't keep up with you."

"Keep me in sight," Cleve ordered.

"You're pulling away."

"Goddamn it, stay with me!"

"I've got a hung tank. I can't."

Now he could see that he was closing the distance between himself and the MIG. He looked back quickly. Pell was falling behind, as far back as Cleve was from the MIG.

"Try shaking it off," Cleve said.

"It won't come off."

"Try again," he said angrily.

He watched the MIG. The smoke had almost stopped, but he was still drawing closer to it. There was no question about that. He had nearly halved the original distance already.

"I can't get it off, Black Lead," Pell complained.

There was only one thing to do.

"Go home, Pell," he said. "Get out of the area."

There was no answer. Cleve looked back. He could not see any wingman. Finally he made him out, far behind.

"Did you get that, Black Two?"

"There's twelve MIGs back here," Pell said clearly.

"Get out of there, Pell. Head for home."

"Do you have me in sight, Cleve?"

"Negative. Withdraw, Pell! That's an order."

"I can't. You'd better come back here."

There was a pause.

"Oh, oh," Pell said.

Cleve looked at the MIG. He was very close to it, almost close enough to fire. He could not have been more than two thousand feet behind it, and just about level. It was only a matter of a little more time, perhaps twenty seconds or thirty. He began lining up to fire, leaning into the moment of climax.

". . . two of them on me," he heard Pell shout. "Do you have me yet, Lead?"

"Negative."

"Outmaneuver them, Pell," somebody interrupted icily. It sounded like DeLeo.

". . . can't turn with this tank on . . ."

Cleve sat watching the ship grow very slowly in his gunsight. "He's outturning me!" Pell cried. "Cleve!"

Before he even answered, Cleve began turning back. He had not fired.

"Don't let them get away, Pell," he said coldly, "I'm on the way now."

He looked over his shoulder. He had not completed ninety degrees of turn, but the MIG was already disappearing rapidly, sailing off into the size of a ship he would not see again, shrinking to a speck. When he rolled out, he glanced back once more. It was gone. He searched the sky ahead to find Pell.

"How high are you, Pell?"

He heard no reply.

"Pell, what altitude are you at?"

"Thirty-eight, no, twenty-eight, twenty-seven thousand! I can't shake him! He's turning inside me!" It was a clear, chilling voice.

Cleve trimmed the nose down. They were slightly below him. He was at thirty-three.

"Where are you, Pell?" somebody in another flight called.

There was the noise of overlapping transmissions.

"Did you get that?" somebody shouted.

"Negative."

Just then Cleve saw two ships, or three, off to his left and low, turning with each other. He rolled down toward them, straining to be able to identify them at the earliest moment. They were still too far off, as anonymous as insects.

"What's your position, Pell?" somebody asked again.

They were MIGs, two MIGs and Pell's ship. Cleve could see them positively now. He looked high, but he did not notice any others above him. He looked behind himself, on both sides.

"It just came off," Pell shouted. "I got rid of the tank!"

"Somebody tell me where he is."

"About ten miles east of Antung," Cleve said.

"Thanks."

Suddenly, as he was diving down toward them, Cleve saw the MIG immediately behind Pell snap and begin to spin. The pilot had pulled too hard to stay in the tighter turn. It was common enough with inexperience. Cleve looked for the second MIG. It took him a moment to pick it up again. He could not tell at first, but then he was certain. It was going away. He could not catch it. He started a turn to keep Pell in sight. Did he see it? Pell was shouting. He was turning outside the spinning MIG, ready to close. Cleve watched the MIG spin down from twenty-five thousand feet, leisurely, like a piece of paper. A parachute finally appeared. Even after that, it seemed minutes before, in some wooded hills, the shadow of the MIG grew quickly to meet it. There was a soft explosion. The smoke began to rise, gray and leaning.

"Did you see him hit?" Pell shouted.

"Roger."

"Who went in?" It was Imil calling. "Are you all right, Pell?"

"Sure. No sweat."

"Who went in?"

"It was a MIG."

"Did you get one?"

"Roger," Pell said.

"Good show."

Back at Kimpo, at debriefing, the colonel stood with his arm around Pell and his other hand hooked by the thumb in his cartridge belt. At the opposite end of the table, for the short time that he remained, DeLeo was like all the unheard voices of the world. His face was expressionless. He would not say anything. Even under the obligation of that, however, of those who believed in him, Cleve could not bring himself to try to explain. Nothing could possibly have been made different by then, anyway. Pell had credit for the MIG, his third.

They swarmed around him, to be near him because the colonel was, and to hear what had happened. They came to see the magician, to wonder at the sleight of hand and be fascinated by the glibness. Toward the end, in a quiet moment, Pell walked up to Cleve.

"I haven't had a chance to thank you," he said.

"Don't bother."

"If you hadn't come back like you did . . ."

"Forget it, Pell."

". . . I don't know how I'd have gotten that MIG confirmed, I didn't have any film of it, naturally. Of course, somebody else might have seen it crash, but you never know."

Colonel Imil appeared beside Pell.

"Let's go on up and grab some lunch," he said. "How about you, Cleve? Want a ride?"

"No, thanks."

He watched them stroll out together and climb into the jeep. They backed into the road and then lurched away, as the colonel put it into gear.

"What's eating him?" the colonel asked Pell over the clatter.

"He's a little hard to get along with."

"You're the first one that's ever said that."

"It's not just me. It's the whole flight, sir, more or less."

"That's bad."

"I don't think he goes for this combat flying too much, Colonel, if you want to know the real truth."

"Come on, now," Imil denied.

Pell shrugged. There was a silence. The jeep rattled through it.

"It's just too bad you can't have a flight," the colonel mused thoughtfully.

Pell did not reply. He preferred to leave that hanging, unadorned, in the air. Later, when he returned to the room, he found Cleve writing a letter. He drew a chair close to the table and sat down. Cleve did not look up.

"Dutch certainly thinks a lot of you," Pell said.

"Some other time, Pell. I'm busy."

"He thinks you've got the best flight in the group," Pell continued. "He said that more than once."

"That's good."

"You knew him before this, didn't you? In Panama."

"Not as intimately as you do. I used to call him Colonel Imil."

"Oh, I don't call him Dutch to his face."

Cleve went on writing.

"He mentioned that he'd known you for a long time," Pell said. "He thinks you're going to get MIGs, too. He has a lot of confidence in you."

"Where do you get your nerve?"

"I mean it."

Cleve said nothing.

"I think he'd like to see me leading elements now instead of flying wing," Pell continued. "He asked about that."

"What did you tell him?"

"I said I thought I would be after I told you about it."

"Well, go back and tell him you were wrong," Cleve said, "because you're in my flight, and you'll be a wingman until I say otherwise. If you ever lead, it will be when I think you're able to."

"Maybe."

"Don't talk to me like that. Not maybe. Absolutely."

"Afraid of what I might do if I had the chance?"

"Get out of here," Cleve ordered.

Pell smiled. He stood up, not in the least awkwardly, and left the room.

Cleve sat at the table for a time without moving. Then he tore the letter he was writing into pieces and threw them away.

18

The fresh days had arrived, the high winds. A sweep of seasons was rustling across the peninsula. It was a clamorous spring. The windows rattled incessantly through bright hours, and doors were ripped open when the wind slipped behind them. Through the rolling hills toward Seoul the scrub pine and occasional willows now seemed to shine. Everywhere were plots of ground that had been carved out and plowed. The earth looked rich but worn in the sunlight. Beside huts along the road the first signs advertising ice for sale appeared. The Koreans cut blocks of it out of the river all winter long and buried it in sawdust to sell when the weather turned hot. It was among the most abundant of their crops.

Daughters's heart was no longer with them, but in the future, ten, nine, eight missions away. He had finished with the war, except in fact. The days were intolerably long for him. Even dreams could not fill them. He thought of nothing now but his sons and his wife, yearning to be with them again. He had cherished at one time, like the rest of them, visions of glory, but they had faded at last and seemed pale indeed beside the prospect of going home.

Daughters had succumbed. He was strolling with his sons

through summer afternoons, taking them to streams and lakes he knew, showing them where the trout hid, the bass.

When he had been a boy himself, he had loved the fields best. He was always keeping animals he found while wandering home from school on autumn afternoons. Spring and summer, too, it was turtles and rabbits, snakes in a burlap bag, field mice, ducks, and dogs. Once it was three young hawks stolen from their nest. He trained them to his hand. When he went to college, the animals in the backyard remembered him from one holiday to the next.

The war took him away, and then marriage. When he was gone for good, his family set everything free. The rabbits went back into the meadows, the snakes slithered off, the field mice and chipmunks vanished, the turtles sunned their withered extremities in their old ponds. The hawks flew away to hunt for themselves. In letters from home, sometimes he would hear about them. They were the only ones that came back, returning singly to perch for a haughty minute or two on the backyard fence, recognizable by the peculiar, jerky movements of their heads. He often felt they were still his.

Something about him made Chung, the houseboy, approach him more readily than any of the others, head bowed, talking in small, uncertain English. Chung. Even Daughters did not know his surname. He was only Chung, always dressed in discarded fatigues with everything too big for his thin frame. The sleeves were turned up, and the trousers, and his feet must have rattled within the heavy field shoes. He came from somewhere, some broken family, some hut in a poor village. They hardly noticed him as the days went by. He seldom spoke. He worked shyly. He shined shoes, made beds, washed glasses, swept floors, cleaned windows, scrubbed, polished, and dusted, and sometimes, when his work was finished, emerged from his unblinking timidity to play catch with the other houseboys. Off to the rear of the area, where they were not seen, they had erected a kind of chinning bar, and he might be there with them, laughing over things said in their own, birdlike language, competing with them in various contests. A call, however, and he would come immediately, throwing down the ball, or slipping on his jacket and leaving the chinning bar to come running. He was there every day from about eight in the morning until five at night. Where he ate or what, Cleve did not know. Sometimes they would give him a couple of candy bars, and though he might have been pleased to receive them, there was no telling from the poised, wide-eyed expression whether he took them out of politeness or with real gratitude. He was a strange boy, a tamed animal in many ways, and in others pitifully human and poor.

"He wants to go home for a few days, Cleve," Daughters explained.

"Where's your home, Chung?"

"Ansong."

"Where's that, Jim?" Cleve asked.

"About fifty miles south of here," Daughters said.

"That's a long way."

Chung did not say anything. He looked at Cleve for a minute out of huge, dark eyes that it suddenly seemed might fill with tears, and then stared at the floor, resignedly.

"How many days, Chung?" Cleve asked.

"Two for walk to home, then two, then two for walk to here.

"Six days."

"Do you want to let him go?" Daughters said.

"He deserves it."

"I think so. He's the best houseboy around here. Aren't you, Chung?"

The boy smiled bashfully. He looked at Cleve.

"There's nothing wrong at home, is there?" Cleve asked.

He shook his head.

"Is your father sick?"

"No father."

"Oh. Your mother?"

"No."

"Why do you want to go?"

"It's his grandfather's birthday," Daughters interrupted.

"And he's going to walk all the way to Ansong? Is that the only reason, Chung?"

"Yes, sir." He looked at the floor.

"All right," Cleve said. "They're your feet."

He went to his shelves and got two packages of cigarettes.

"Here. Presento. For your grandfather, you understand?"

The boy took them without any evidence of pleasure. Cleve felt moved to add something else that might be appreciated more. He reached into his pocket and took out some money. He counted it, eight thousand wuan in all. Chung was paid thirty thousand a month.

"Here, take this, too. You might need it," Cleve said.

The boy did not want to accept it. Cleve forced it into the small, callused hand.

Chung kept everything he used or owned on the ledge of the window, and after Cleve had gone, he laid the cigarettes there on a piece of unfolded cloth. Pell happened to notice them when he came in. He had been down at the firing-in range with Hunter, checking the guns on his own ship. He had come to consider himself quite a gunner and liked to be present to supervise every detail. It was the same with the inspections of his airplane. Pell would discuss the fine points of maintenance with his crew chief, who was fortunately very voluble, while Pettibone or Hunter stood by and waited for him, but listening. He was a little like those golfers who are expert enough to refine the balance of their clubs with minuscule dabs of lead, and, regardless of what he knew, he was busily improving his dialogue all the time.

As he came in the door, he stopped to stare at the contents of Chung's handkerchief.

"What's he doing with the cigarettes?" he asked. "Whose are they?"

"Cleve gave them to him," Daughters said.

"What in hell for? The only good thing about him was that he didn't smoke."

"They're a birthday present for his grandfather. He's going home on leave."

"Leave? Who let him have that?"

"Cleve."

"And a present, too, eh?" Pell thought about it for a moment and then opened the door. "Chung!"

The boy appeared quickly from around a corner.

"What's this about your grandfather's birthday? Is that right?"

"Yes, sir."

"You're taking a leave for that?"

"Yes, sir."

"You don't even have a grandfather, Chung," Pell accused.

The boy stood silent and confused.

"Come on, Chung. Who are you trying to fool? You've probably got some twelve-year-old lined up that you're aching to slip it into. Isn't that right?"

"I not know, sir. I go see my grandfather."

"Sure," Pell said, "and you're bringing your grandfather two packs of cigarettes."

The boy nodded. His tiny hands hung nervously at his side. The round, placid face did not know what expression to assume. The beadlike eyes searched questioningly. It seemed that he was preparing himself to give back the cigarettes as if he had expected that all along, that someone would take them from him.

"Don't look so scared," Pell ordered. "She smokes, too, eh?"

"I not know."

"Do you have a carton, Billy Lee?"

"Sure."

"Let me have them. I'll buy you some this afternoon."

Pell took the carton and gave it to the boy.

"Here," he said. "Here's some cigarettes. You'd better take some C rations, too."

Pell pulled out an open case and found tea, sugar, coffee, and other staples. He made a stack of them.

"There's some real presents for you," Pell said. "She ought to give you some number-one loving for them."

Chung cast a questioning glance toward Daughters.

"What are you looking at him for? I'm giving it to you. You don't have to get anybody's permission. Mine is all you need. Understand?"

"Yes, sir."

"Go ahead then. Wrap them up."

The boy carried everything to the window and began to stow

it neatly in his cloth. The two packages of cigarettes that had been there originally were lost in the comparative wealth of dry goods.

"Christ," Pell announced, "could he spare it? Two lousy packages of cigarettes. Next time you want anything around here, Chung, you know who to see, don't you?"

Daughters walked outside and sat in the sunlight alone. He was troubled. He fought against it. He was only serving out a sentence now and would soon be free. He was putting days behind him like miles, pushing them underneath, and his gaze was only forward. Nothing, no cry for help, no shouting, no clamor could have caused him to turn it elsewhere. He was looking toward home and the end of his war. The terrible excitement was no longer compelling. The tightness of the stomach when he was in the sky was like sickness. He could not have been made to stay for even the holiest of reasons. When he had done his tour, he would be released, and he was drawing close to that, unbearably close. The rending of the flight he did not recognize. He would have denied it, as a matter of fact. He would have said that it did not exist. He could not afford to be involved, and to protect himself he had grown to believe there was no such thing. But that afternoon he had been moved to want to talk to Cleve, to say something important to him, he did not know exactly what, since he had blinded himself to the realities of the situation for so long. There was something in him, though, some unsubmerged faculty that made him know, with what he felt must be instinct, that he had to try.

He found a chance that night in the bar. It was a warm, vagrant evening. Spring attacked the blood like a virus. Cleve was talking to Nolan, getting the schedule for the next day. Four missions for the squadron. Three that his flight would go on. The first one was at 0700, then 1030 and 1400.

"Do you feel like going on all three of them, Jim?"

"I'd like to."

"0700 is the early-morning reconnaissance," Nolan explained.

"And the other two?"

"Both sweeps."

Cleve nodded. Those were the ones he would go on.

"All right," he said. "It's you and Pell on the reccy, Jim. Bert and Pettibone, too."

"What time is the briefing?" Daughters asked.

"O five fifty," Nolan said.

Daughters grinned.

"You can sleep during the mission," Cleve said. "You won't see anything."

"They've been up that early."

"Not often."

"No, but when Pell got his second MIG, it was on an early-morning mission, remember?"

"I remember."

"They ought to be flying sometime tomorrow," Nolan said, as he moved off. "They've been up every day now for six days."

That was the speculation the club buzzed with nightly. A contagious note of anticipation was steady in the air. Through it all, as the older pilots argued about tactics or personalities, and the new men who had yet to see the enemy sat in forced silence, listening to stories of great battles that had taken place in the past and increased in ferocity with the passage of time, the name kept coming up, the loving description of the ship shining inviolable, striped in defiance. He had returned, and they might encounter him any time, in the brightness of a spring noon perhaps, suddenly, unannounced, like a heavy angel come down to test the valor of men.

"Whoever gets him," Imil was supposed to have said, "is going to have to be a better pilot than I am, and I don't know if any of you boys are."

It was a typical Imil story.

"I wanted to talk to you, Cleve," Daughters said.

"What's on your mind?"

"Pell."

"Is that all?"

"What do you mean?"

"I'm not interested. Talk about something else. Do you know what they're talking about here? I've been listening to it for an hour."

"I know how you gave up a kill to go and help him. I'm not the only one, either."

"He got the MIG."

"What's that?"

"More than a mouthful of ashes," Cleve said.

"When this is over, he'll be nothing. You know that, don't you?"

"And what about us? What will we be?"

"That's not the point," Daughters said. "His getting that MIG was just an accident."

"It doesn't matter. He got it."

"You'll have your chances, Cleve, plenty of them to make up for it."

"Sure, I suppose I will." There was always that, right up to the end.

He had come prepared to acquit himself, but now he was not sure. He had come for a climax of victory, but in a way he did not want that now. He wanted more, to be above wanting it, to be independent of having to have it. And he knew, with the utmost certainty, he would never achieve that. He was a prisoner of the war. If he did not get MIGs he would have failed, not only in his own eyes but in everyone's. Talking to DeLeo, to Daughters, to anybody, it was only too plain. They said it meant nothing, but their denials were a confession. They expected something from him. He was the old hand.

He would have seized anything that allowed him release. He dreaded the need of sacrificing himself on this pitiless altar, of fighting for something he no longer had the strength to disdain: a place beside the next ace in the group. Pell.

19

In the early morning he heard them rise. He lay there more asleep than awake, listening to the scraping of shoes and the creaking of cots as they dressed in silence or with occasional whispers. Then one by one they left, until finally the door slammed shut for the last time. He passed into grateful sleep again, and it seemed a long while, hours later, before he was aware of the sound of their engines opening full, cremating the quiet of the first daylight. The noise rolled up from the runway, interminable, wavering in climax, and then gradually diminishing as they released the brakes and accelerated away, trailing their thunder, fainter quickly, then still fainter, then gone. After that he remained awake, thinking unhappily of them, off without him, not abstractly, but as they were in their cockpits: Daughters first, Pell, DeLeo, Pettibone.

After breakfast, he walked down to operations. It was cool, with the promise of heat. Looking to the south, he could see patches of early mist remaining, through which the jagged hills thrust. A trail of dust followed the few vehicles that passed him. Birds darted by. He could hear their frail cries. He walked along somnambulantly, lulled by concern. He looked at his watch. The flight was on the way back now, he calculated. They were probably starting to let down the long, invisible slope of sky that peaked fifty or sixty miles north. He passed through the maintenance area. Crewmen were working on the ships, preparing them for a full day of missions. He inspected the sky appraisingly, for the first time. It was going to be fair. The sun was climbing and becoming just strong enough to be felt, like a layer of cloth.

Somebody came running by and shouted to him. He turned his head. He stopped walking as the words registered. Had he heard about the reccy flight?

"What about it?"

The man called over his shoulder, going away.

"They ran into MIGs. They got two."

Unconsciously, he looked up at the empty sky for a moment, as if in supplication, as the sudden, fierce anguish hit him. Everything he had suffered in the past came flooding back, stronger than ever. He was afraid to learn the rest. It would have done no good to ask, anyway. The man had run on. He had just reached the operations building when he heard them a few minutes later. He looked up, searching. Then he saw them. They were about to enter on initial. He watched incredulously. It was like seeing a man without a head approaching. There were only three ships.

He walked out into the parking area and stood there to wait for them. He could not tell anything from where he was as they flew their pattern, and further, the walls of sandbags and lines of airplanes blocked his view of the runway. Quite a few people were moving out, independently, into the parking area to observe, too. A long period of time seemed to have passed since they had landed. At last he heard the faint whistle characteristic of engines idling. It grew louder. He watched. The first ship swung evenly into the open area, followed closely by the other two. He recognized their helmets as they went by. It was DeLeo in the first airplane. Pettibone in the second. In the third was Pell. Cleve began running. He reached DeLeo's ship just as it came to a stop, and jumped up on the wing. There was a whining deflation as DeLeo shut down his engine and slowly, not looking at Cleve although he knew he was there, removed his helmet and saddled it on the windshield.

"What happened?" Cleve asked.

"We ran into Casey. Christ! I've never . . ."

"Where?"

"I don't know—coming back. I wouldn't have believed it. I swear to God," DeLeo breathed.

"What about Daughters?"

"He got hit."

"How?"

"I don't know." He stood up on the seat, bending over to fumble with the parachute buckles. "He went straight in." His knees were shaking.

"Did you see it?"

DeLeo threw his leg over the side of the ship and stepped down onto the wing. He steadied himself there. A small group of crewmen and some officers were gathering below.

"Yes, I saw him. Anybody within ten miles saw him. He was on fire. You couldn't miss him."

"Are you sure he didn't get out?"

"No, we would have seen it," DeLeo said. He slid himself

down from the wing and made his way through the thin crowd, ignoring the questioners, toward the revetment where Pell was parked. Cleve walked beside him.

"Who got the MIGs, Bert?"

"Pell."

Cleve stopped walking abruptly.

"Wait," he said. "Did you see that, too?"

"I saw one of them hit."

"How did it happen? I want to know."

They stood in the middle of the ramp, looking at the pierced steel planking underfoot, and sometimes at each other. DeLeo told it haltingly. They had completed their reconnaissance and were headed south when the MIGs hit them. It was Casey Jones and five others, a complete surprise. Nobody had seen them until they were close in, firing. Nobody had heard any warning. Then, in the break, they were separated.

"All the stories, you know?" DeLeo said. "They're nothing. Not even a beginning. Jesus! No matter what I did. I even gave up, I swear. I sat there waiting. He was behind me the whole time. I almost tore the wings off trying to lose him. It didn't matter. He stayed there. I just can't tell you. The funny thing, he never fired. At least I never saw it. He just stayed in back of me. I don't know how I got away. He could have had me a dozen times. Right from the start, but he never fired. I guess it was his guns. It must have been. All the time Pettibone was screaming to turn tighter. I don't know where the hell he was. I never saw him. A lot of help, that kid. I'd have done better alone. At the end I heard Pell calling to Daughters to bail out and Pettibone asking where everybody was. I finally caught sight of this smoke. Daughters.

His ship was on fire, streaming fuel. I saw it hit. Then another one, closer. Christ! I was sure it was Pettibone. It turned out to be one of them."

There was a crowd around Pell's ship, and in the midst of it, as they drew closer, they could see him gesturing. Somebody asked DeLeo if he had gotten any. He did not answer. He pushed through. Then Pell saw them and began shaking his head apologetically.

"It happened so quick," Pell said, "he didn't have a chance. Two of them just popped up between us. They started hitting him right away. I got both of them finally, but it was too late."

"Why didn't you call a break?" DeLeo asked.

"I did."

"Like hell you did. I didn't hear it."

"I called him two or three times," Pell protested.

"You're lying."

"You couldn't have been looking around much, if two MIGs got in on him like that," Cleve said.

"We were in a fight. When you're going around with them, there can always be more of them behind you somewhere."

"Never mind the fundamentals."

"I'm just trying to explain," Pell shrugged.

"You were supposed to be clearing him."

"I was. I called the break as soon as I saw them," Pell replied, "but he didn't break. What would you have done? I started shooting to get them off his tail."

"I would have gotten him back," Cleve said.

"Oh, come off it. I feel bad enough as it is. What good does this do?"

"No good," Cleve said, "but you're through, Pell. You've gone your own way for the last time. There won't be another. I promise you that."

Pell was not apparently disturbed. Instead, he seemed almost relieved to hear it. The open concern fell away, and on his face appeared the old, sly confidence.

"You weren't even there," he said. "How do you know what happened? You were in bed. You're always off somewhere when there's a fight, in Tokyo or someplace."

"Am I?"

It was as if some capsule had been squeezed open within him and the contents shot into his blood like venom. He stepped unthinkingly forward, unbalanced, but quickly, his hands feeling weightless as he moved. His swing did not hit Pell squarely, but glanced off the side of the neck. A surge of bodies closed in upon them immediately, crowding them so that he could not move his arms, one of which was caught shoulder high. There was shouting and confusion as he was forced back clumsily.

"What in hell is going on here?"

It was Colonel Imil, pushing brusquely through the group. He glanced around and then turned on Cleve.

"All right. What is it? What's the trouble?"

"Nothing."

"What do you mean, nothing?" He looked toward Pell. "Haven't you had enough fighting for one day?"

Pell smiled.

"You got two more, I hear," the colonel said.

"Yes, sir."

"Who was lost?"

"Daughters."

"How did it happen?"

"He just got hit," Pell began. "I did everything I could . . ."

"Colonel," Cleve said, his breath making him pause, "I'd like to talk to you alone for a minute."

"What about?"

"I'd rather tell you alone."

"What's bothering you, Cleve? Say it out in the open. What are you afraid of?"

The color came to Cleve's face. He could feel his mouth hardening despite himself. The hands of the crowd had released him, and he stood by himself, conscious of the surrounding faces now withdrawn slightly to a respectful distance, but silent and absorbing. He abandoned the search for proper words.

"I want Pell grounded," he said.

The silence, which had been noticeable, became paramount when the colonel did not immediately reply. It was the silence of the arena.

"What in hell are you talking about?"

"Ground him," Cleve repeated. "I want to see that he doesn't fly any more."

"A man with five victories, and you want me to ground him? What's wrong with you? He ought to be a flight commander."

"Why not give him the group, Colonel?"

"That's enough, Connell."

"He killed his leader today. If he'd shot him down personally, it wouldn't have been any different. It was his fault that Daughters was killed."

"It wasn't my fault," Pell insisted. "He wouldn't break."

"You're a liar. You never told him to."

The colonel suddenly jerked his head up and looked around at the rows of open faces. He wheeled toward them.

"All right," he shouted, scattering them with motions of his hands, "go on about your business, all of you. Clear out of here."

They began to filter away. He stood watching until they were gone. Then he turned to DeLeo and Pell.

"Get to debriefing. They're waiting for your report."

"I have a right to hear what he says," Pell announced.

"Don't worry about that," the colonel ordered. "Just get going."

Pell saluted, and then, belatedly, DeLeo. When they were some distance off, and only he, Cleve, and Moncavage were left standing by the wing of Pell's ship, the colonel whirled to confront Cleve with unexpected ferocity.

"What are you trying to do, Connell? Wreck the group?"

"No, sir. I'm trying to uphold it."

"With crazy accusations in front of every son of a bitch and his brother?"

"I was told to speak in front of them," Cleve said flatly.

"First of all," the colonel continued with a rush, not listening, "you weren't even on the mission—why, I don't know. I only know that there's nothing unusual about it. You never seem to be on the missions that get into fights. That's the first thing. Secondly, for some reason, you and that Italian, whatever his name is, have got it in for Pell, but if it weren't for him, and nobody else, your flight would be on its ass. Nobody else in it is doing a thing except him. I hate to lose a pilot and a plane, probably more than anybody else around here, but I don't jump to conclusions. I'll find out what went on; and if I think there was anything that requires action on my part, I'll take it. I don't have to be told by some captain how to run my wing or who to ground."

"How long have you known me, Colonel?"

"I don't care if I've known you for fifty years."

"Just listen to me for a minute."

"No! That's what you can't seem to understand. You listen to me. I don't listen to you."

"On whatever reputation . . ." Cleve began.

"At ease! Are you too stupid to understand that?"

Cleve did not reply. He was looking at a stranger, complete and hostile. Whatever the mutual past had given them was suddenly gone. It was a sickening feeling to realize that, like having the very ground taken from beneath his feet. He did not remember later whether anything more had been said, but only that he had been left standing alone beside Pell's airplane, the fury slowly subsiding and leaving him stranded more and more on the outcropping of complete loneliness and desolation. He did not know what to do. He could not even think clearly about it. In the middle of the ramp he was left by himself. He would have given anything to be gone, years away. It would be a long time, though, before he was finished here and could begin putting it behind him. He had days ahead that seemed like mountain ranges.

Pell faced the colonels in the debriefing room. He was earnest and attentive. He looked directly at them when he answered their questions. It didn't take long. After about ten minutes he was finished explaining, and they all left to drive up to the club. It was closed at that hour, but Moncavage located the club officer and borrowed the keys.

They walked in together. It was empty and cool, like a kitchen at midnight. They sat down at the bar. Moncavage found the right key for the liquor cabinet and withdrew a bottle.

"There're some glasses right in back of you," Imil said. Moncavage placed three out. Imil picked the cork from the bottle and poured them about one quarter full.

"You probably need this," he said to Pell, "and it won't hurt me."

Moncavage was trying to find some water to mix with his drink.

"A big day. Here's to you, Doctor," Imil said, lifting his glass.

He and Pell drank, swallowing hurriedly.

"Phew," Imil breathed. He set his teeth against each other. "Still a little early in the morning."

Pell laughed and wiped his mouth.

"I must be getting old," Imil said. "How about you, Monk?"

Moncavage was just taking a sip from his glass.

"It isn't orange juice," he said.

"Drink it."

They sat around, drinking slowly. The sun came through the windows, making squares of brilliance on the rough wood flooring. Other than that, the room was dim. The walls were indistinct in shadow. Pell could feel the liquor moving through him. He hadn't eaten any breakfast. Imil took the bottle and poured him another one, taking a little himself.

"Two MIGs in one mission," he said. "That's something."

"I got a couple on one mission, myself," Moncavage said.

"You did, didn't you?" Imil agreed. "Well, you ought to form a club."

Pell grinned.

"That's the way to do it, though," Imil went on. "Christ, it's all most of us can manage just to get one. You boys that deal in pairs. I don't know."

He inspected his glass closely.

"I'll tell you something, though," he said to Pell. "As long as you live, no matter what happens, you'll never forget this."

"No, sir."

"The day you made ace."

Pell emptied his glass to that. He could feel a general looseness coming on.

"Colonel," he began sturdily.

"What?"

"You're right. I'll never forget it."

"Hell, no."

"What about you?"

"Forget my fifth kill?"

"Yeah," Pell nodded, almost as if a difficult point had been resolved.

"The first time or the second? Ah, it doesn't make any difference. I remember both of them. Especially that first, though. How old are you, Doctor?"

"Twenty-five." Pell spread the fingers of one hand out slowly on the bar as if consulting them.

"Twenty-five."

Pell nodded.

"Do you know how old I was when I got my fifth?" Imil asked.

"No."

"Twenty-two."

"Just a kid," Pell said, smiling.

Imil laughed. When drinking, he seemed bigger than ever. He licked his lips.

"I remember it like yesterday. England. Now there was a war—right, Monk?"

"I was in Italy."

"Tough." He drained his glass and watched as Pell tried to fill them all evenly again. "I remember when I came down that day. What a feeling! The whole world wasn't big enough for me. You know what I mean."

"Right," Pell agreed impulsively.

"I had this girl. Know what she said?"

"No."

" 'Be a bloody ace tonight, that's all.' " He held his fist and forearm up and laughed.

Pell shrugged happily.

"It's what everybody thinks," he muttered.

The sound of engines being run up filled the room slowly. They stared toward the window. A mission was leaving. They could see the ships marshaled on the end of the runway.

"Look at that," Imil said.

They watched intently. The first ships started to go, and the air in the room trembled.

"There go your boys, Monk," Imil cried, sweeping a hand in their direction. He upset his glass. The drink spilled out over the bar. He ignored it. "Gives you the feeling, doesn't it?"

Moncavage agreed.

"Always does when you don't have to go," Imil said. He knocked the overturned glass to the floor with an abrupt movement. It bounced to the wall but did not break. Moncavage reached behind and got another one out.

The noise of engines finally receded. Pell was leaning on both elbows. He stirred himself to wave a hand meaninglessly.

"The way it is," he said indistinctly.

"What?"

"You know," Pell said. "I thought of something."

"What is it?"

"His receiver could have been out," Pell said. "Right?"

"Ah, forget that. It's finished with."

"Is it? Really?"

"You did the best you could," Imil said. "It was one of those things, that's all."

"I did call him."

"Look. You got two MIGs, didn't you?"

Pell pulled at an imaginary trigger. He made a sound with his tongue like guns firing.

"Hosed 'em," he said. "That's the important part, isn't it? What's so hard to believe?"

There was a silence.

"He should've been looking around," Pell said. "He'd have seen 'em if he was. You'd have seen 'em, Colonel."

"Forget it, Pell."

"I don't know what they told you," Pell said slowly. He was very serious. "But this is a fact. Just want to get this one thing straight. I called him."

Imil picked up the bottle and dumped another drink out for the three of them. He paused. Then he began evenly.

"Listen," he said, "you've got five kills."

"Right," Pell cried fiercely.

"That's a real distinction."

"I know."

"People'll remember that as long as you live. They'll point you out. Understand?"

"Damned right."

"Well, don't forget it, Pell. Remember what you are."

"You and me, Colonel."

Imil drew an audible breath.

"That's right, isn't it?" Pell asked.

"Yeah."

"Couple aces," Pell laughed.

The colonel stared at him, but Pell didn't seem to notice. "You know you'll be going to Tokyo this afternoon," Imil explained in a different tone.

"Roge."

"Shaking hands with all the generals. You understand."

"Shake hell out of 'em."

"You stay there three or four days, anyway," Imil ordered. "Get everything off your mind, you know?"

"Sure."

"Come back when you feel like it."

"Don't worry," Pell said.

There was not much talking then, until the glasses were empty; and after Pell had gotten to his feet and made his way to the door, none. Imil watched him leave. He looked briefly at Moncavage and then turned further to stare out the window through which they had seen the ships taking off.

"Well, what are you going to do?" Moncavage asked at last. He was inwardly pleased at the whole affair.

"You're the group commander. What are your ideas?"

"I don't know."

"Neither do I."

"Do you still believe him?"

"I don't know," Imil hedged. "It's the same as what I told him, though. He's an ace. We might as well be proud of it."

Pell left for Tokyo that afternoon to be interviewed by the press and Headquarters people. Hunter and Pettibone went with him. The colonel had granted them permission to take leave and go, too. Pell had requested it, and though it was an unusual thing to ask for, it had been arranged so promptly that the three of them were aboard an airplane for Japan long before the customary telegram from General Muehlke arrived. This was delivered to the room at about five o'clock, a yellow sheet of teletype paper beginning: PERSONAL FROM MUEHLKE TO PELL. It continued with congratulations on Pell's becoming an ace. Cleve saw it when he returned after the last mission of the day, which had been uneventful. He picked it up and read it. The late sunlight was coming through the windows in level, clearly defined rays along which dust as fine as smoke floated. DeLeo, tired, too, from the full day of flying, read it over Cleve's shoulder. They said nothing to each other. Cleve tossed it back on the bed.

It was very quiet, the part of the day when time was at top dead center, the hours when everybody always seemed to have gone somewhere. He could hear the gentle fluttering of the damper in the stovepipe as the wind moved it. He was tired. His body felt as if it were wrapped uncomfortably in his skin. He took off most of his clothes and lay down on top of the blanket on his cot. Suddenly he was very mortal. The sun coming through the window warmed his face and chest, where the band of it fell upon him. He closed his eyes. They were dry, but slowly the fluid came to soothe them. The sun felt good. It lay like a balm on flesh that was so easily pierced and torn. It smoothed out the perspective of life somehow. His thoughts drifted free.

And his heart ached for Daughters. He could feel, as if it were happening to himself at that moment, the last terrible anguish as the dark, vacant maw of the MIG swung in behind, fat and merciless, pumping out shells, the lashes of tracer sailing past like high voltage or third rails to be touched by. He shrank as Daughters must have to avoid them, straining to look back, turning hard but too late through the heavy fire. Perhaps he had been hit in the cockpit. If that were true, it would not have been too bad. A man was small in the airplane, though. He might not have been hit when his ship was, but have been trapped instead, sitting there fighting the gone controls, the airspeed winding up higher and higher, the green earth rushing fast to meet him. On a warm day, and all alone, it was not easy to die. Death could be slighted or even ignored close by; but when the time came to meet it unexpectedly, no man could find it in himself not to cry silently or aloud for just one more reprieve to keep the world from ending.

His thoughts lingered over his own chances to live. It was not the first time, but he had never been so isolated before, so open to the tortures of imagination. Every contact, from the lieutenants he led to the commanders he followed, had been severed. The reputation he had worn so lightly had vanished into dust, and with it any strength he had drawn from disdaining it. He felt assailed from every side and unable to force his thoughts away from himself. The difficult thing to think about was having to bail out deep in North Korea and being hunted in enemy country. What mattered most in a case like that was the sustained will to live, much different from the instinctive will. He was not sure he had enough of that in him any more to survive, if it happened to him. It was like being a hemophiliac and competing for a boxing championship. He listened to the hordes of sparrows chattering under the eaves. Spring, he thought, and then all of a long summer.

And Casey Jones. He thought of him. He had questioned DeLeo dry and for the first time felt the possession of hard knowledge, the thrill and disappointment of finding an enemy to be human. Alone now, retreating, hating them all, drawing off as if down a long corridor continuous but concealing, away from them and the things they admired, he could almost feel the presence, dark and strong, of his chosen enemy, more than that, his friend. He had never seen him. Imil had, though. DeLeo. It was almost as if he were working closer, along a chain of men. He could not help dreaming of it. Casey Jones, whoever he was, to meet and take him high in the piercing blue of those northern skies, and then to stand up spitefully before them, to earn that gesture, that final voice. He discarded it as narcotic again and again, but it kept returning, one thing of merit, out of anonymity, out of failure. One clean mark for them all to see. To kill a champion. To know once more the breath of excellence, compared to which everything else was dross.

20

Even time stood still for Pell, and the constellations froze. During the five days he was in Tokyo, there was no major fight, hardly even a sighting. The very skies hung quiet while he was gone. When he returned, his accomplishments were still the freshest, his name the most spoken. Everything was exactly as it had been when he left, with one exception. He was not. He had changed. That triumphant week had given him something he had never possessed, a hard luster for his assurance. He had become the final Pell, full grown, immutable. If he had seemed frail, he was no sturdier, but that flicking slightness now had an infrangible quality, like cable. He was established. If still shadowed by the ordinary perils, there was one at least he was now fully beyond: disregard. Everybody knew Pell, and he gloried in it. He drank it, like the can of cold beer that his crew chief would hand up to the cockpit when he taxied in, following a mission at the end of the day. He ate it, beneath his picture in the mess, framed and titled along with those of the other aces there had been, all of them indestructible and dramatic in grays and blacks. He wore it, the aristocratic shield that every man recognized, a line of five red stars painted on his plane just beneath the cockpit.

In the evening they stopped by the room to have a drink and

talk or to hear Pell soliloquize, smoking his cigars. They sat around him, and the smoke rose in a canopy beneath the ceiling. They listened. It had been a george deal, Pell told them. He had met the top brass in Tokyo, the boys who were really running this war. He just wished he'd had the chance to follow up on all the fat leads. There was no telling what couldn't be done. All they had to do was flick the ash off their cigarettes and pick up the telephone to arrange anything, and they were all calling him Doctor. There was this admiral, for one, who wanted him to come out to the carriers on a kind of exchange deal and fly with them for a while. The admiral had said he could easily fix the whole thing up with the commander of the carrier force, if Pell agreed to do it. A few strings might have to be pulled, of course, but it could be arranged. The colonels who were handling things for him in Tokyo didn't think too much of the idea, though, Pell said. One of them wanted him to finish his tour and then go into operations in the States. He would get him a good job in Air Defense Command Headquarters. They needed someone who knew the fighter business, and there was a good future in it, quick promotion and all that.

"I told him I'd think it over," Pell explained. "He was an old-timer. I didn't want to make him feel bad."

"What's his name? I wouldn't mind a job like that."

"You wouldn't be in an airplane from one year to the next."

"Maybe not. Who's the colonel, though?"

"Never mind," Pell said. "I'm still thinking it over."

Colonel Imil had already advised him to continue in a tactical unit when he finished up in Korea. That was good advice, Pell admitted, but it was hard to be sure. It paid to look into everything.

He smoothed his shirt, tucking it in around his belt. Even his uniform seemed to have become distinctive, with the gun belt loose enough so that the loaded holster tugged heavily at his waist and the red satin baseball cap pulled slightly to the side. In a group of any size he could be picked out immediately, even with his back turned. He puffed lightly on the long cigar that was so damaging to illusion. His hands were too effeminate to hold it, and his mouth and face too thin. It was like seeing a jockey with a family.

"We won a few and lost a few, eh, Petti?" Pell said.

Pettibone reddened. He had been quieter than usual since the return.

"How's the old wound?" Pell asked.

"Never mind."

"Don't be that way. Everybody's interested."

"Oh, lay off, will you?"

"Let's have a look," Pell insisted. "Get under the light here."

"No."

"Don't be like a girl. What are you so shy about?"

"Nothing."

"You showed it to at least half of Tokyo."

"Come on, Petti," someone joined in.

"Lay it on the table."

"Why don't you cut it out?" Pettibone said unhappily.

In Tokyo, Pell had gotten him a woman for the first time in his life. It had been in some rambling hotel in the middle of the night, and there had been a great commotion in Pettibone's room. They rushed to see what it was. When they entered, he was standing testily in the center of the room in only his shorts. Blood was running down his leg. Stains of it were all over the floor and his clothing. Somehow he had split his foreskin, it developed, and he stood there not knowing what to do, while the girl ran for help. In the midst of the confusion, she returned with the hotel manager and others, most of them girls. They stood observing closely, until some bandages were brought. Everyone served as a consultant, examining the progress, and it was almost an hour before the room was cleared.

It was a great story, very funny. Pell told it to everybody. There were stories about him, too, of course. He attracted numbers of them, as a magnet affects metal filings. A whole train of legends had begun to appear.

Hunter spread them. Everything that Pell had said and done he amplified, especially the reception in Tokyo. Actually, he admitted, they had not seen too much of him. It had been a tight program. In the evenings, though, they heard a recounting of who he had been in to see, what he had told them, and what was in the offing. Pell saw nobody but generals, Hunter said. An admiral or two, maybe. He even put in a few good words for the flight, for all of them, Hunter emphasized, with General Muehlke himself. He spent a whole afternoon in the general's office while colonels waited outside.

The inaccuracies were greater at the club, and when Pettibone came in, he was loudly greeted now.

"Lover!" they called out when they saw him. "Stud!"

Colonel Moncavage stood up and promised he would get the Purple Heart for Pettibone, if proof of injury were shown at the bar. There was a roar of approval and cheers for Pettibone.

"Lay it out there," somebody urged.

"Show him the stitches."

Pettibone looked at the floor, flushed and speechless. He yearned for the presence of mind to say something cutting.

"Weren't any stitches. Pell exaggerates everything," he murmured.

"You want the Purple Heart?" the colonel said. "Come on."

The more Cleve saw of it, the more withdrawn he became. Daily, hourly, building up after every mission, during the talks with DeLeo, the evenings in the club, the nights in bed, running through the mind like a stream through the earth, cutting a path for itself, increasing in intensity, growing, dominating everything he did on the major plane of life, he hated Pell. He hated him in a way that allowed no other emotion. It seemed he was born to, and that he had done it from the earliest days of his life, before he ever knew him, before he even existed. Of all the absolutes, Pell was the archetype, confronting him with the unreality and diabolical force of a medieval play, the deathlike, grinning angel risen to claim the very souls of men. When he dwelt upon that, Cleve felt the cool touch of fear. There was no way out. He knew that if Pell were to win, he himself could not survive.

He lived with uneasiness. In the afternoons it had become hot enough to take a cot outside and lie in the sunshine. The waves of heat rolled up and over, as he lay there fevered and stripped to shorts. The traffic pattern was almost directly above him. With closed eyes, the rushing sound of the ships seemed to swell quickly and then start to fade before they were even overhead. It was a trick of the wind.

The early mornings were bad. He disliked the first-light missions because of it. He was weakest then, in the mornings, naked, with the film of total sleep still coating his eyes and mouth.

He was his true age when he looked into the mirror to shave, and he doubted his own ability.

At night, though, especially if there had been any losses, it was worse. There was the endless fight against imagination. He could not help wondering, weighing chances. He felt beyond all men and places. The States were far away, impossible even to think of. Only to be in Tokyo once more, only that, down the wide avenues in the warm evening, beside the river, through the park. There was no pleasure in the world to equal that, as it passed through his mind like bursts of music. The rich, drunken darkness, he thought, and moving lazily through it in a lurching cab to be again on the clean mat floors at Miyoshi's, to know the deference, the deep, satisfying night.

One afternoon, following a mission, Imil spoke to him for the first time. It was after debriefing. The room was almost empty.

"I've been wanting to talk to you."

Cleve felt the awkwardness, and within himself an excitement that he was instantly ashamed of.

"Let's walk outside," the colonel suggested.

They stood in the sunshine, leaning against the sandbag walls that surrounded the building.

"I've got a lousy temper, Cleve," the colonel said. "I say things I'm sorry for later. I mean them at the time maybe, or I think I do, but then I'm sorry for them."

Cleve said nothing. The colonel looked down at the ground.

"But I'm not a small man. At least there's nobody around here that can call me that." He ventured a smile.

A pair of airmen walked by and saluted. Imil saw them but did not move to return it.

"I made a mistake," he said.

"Yes, sir."

"I'd like you to forget it. If you want to know, I'd probably have done the same thing you did. Acted the same way. But it's all over with now, and I admit I was wrong."

"Yes, sir."

"Is that all?" Imil asked.

"I say things I'm sorry for, too," Cleve replied after a moment.

Imil shrugged to indicate he understood. "Maybe this will be one," Cleve continued. "Colonel, it's not a matter for apologies."

Imil flushed.

"Well, goddamn you," he said angrily. "All right. If that's what you want."

He walked away without saying anything further. Even if Cleve had not realized then how grievous was a wounded, mighty pride, the days that followed made it clear. Imil never approached him again in any way.

DeLeo had only three more missions left to make his hundred, and he was anxious to finish. He would not be happy when he was home, and he knew it; but it did not deter him. Toward the end they all got that way. With the strange, unreasoning quality that puts aside everything to satisfy some fleeting desire, they became transfixed with the thought of finishing and moved to do so as those dying of thirst follow mirages.

"Three trips," DeLeo said. "Three more. Then to hell with it."

"Twenty-five for me," Cleve counted. They were marked on the wall. They seemed like days left to live.

"I'll send you a postcard to keep your morale up."

"Fine."

"Hope you're having a good time. Get one for me. Your admirer, Albert E. DeLeo."

"You'll wish you were back."

"Oh, no. Not even when I'm drunk. It's all yours. I've had this war. Ninety-seven missions and still looking for a damaged. What's the use?"

"You wouldn't be the first who got hot on the last two or three."

"Why kid myself? I'm not having that kind of luck. Neither are you."

This luck or that. They believed in it like gamblers, right from Desmond at the start on those first winter days.

"It isn't luck," Cleve said.

"No? I'd hate to tell you who I heard that from last. Face it, Cleve. You get the breaks or you don't."

"Don't blame the breaks."

"Thanks. You've a lot to be proud of, too."

"I haven't quit," Cleve said.

"It wouldn't make much difference, believe me. It's too late."

"You don't know that."

"Maybe not," DeLeo said. "Maybe I'm stupid. All I know is that I thought once I'd be able to boast: I was in that flight; I was with him; we were together."

There was a long silence, midnight deep.

"It hasn't turned out that way, has it?"

"Oh, Christ. Let's not talk about it. All I want is to be on that schedule tomorrow."

21

On a day with only a few thin stories of clouds high up, like the froth on a great swell, DeLeo went on his final mission. The MIGs came up. When they were announced in the area, he felt as nervous as he had been in his first fight; but neither he nor anybody else saw them; and finally, a little earlier than was necessary, he turned the flight and headed back toward the south. He sat hunched in the cockpit, thinking, his vigilance gone. Although he continued to scan the sky occasionally, he did it with unseeing eyes. He relied on Pettibone's and spent most of the time looking at the ground and out over the enameled surface of the sea.

It was like leaving an old love. There was so much more than he could ever remember. He stared down at the hand-sized earth that had drifted by beneath him so slowly every time before. Now he seemed to be crossing it with great speed, as if running with the current of time. Ribbons of ocher road, highlands and villages were all floating swiftly out of sight under the wing. He felt an overwhelming, captive sadness. It was his farewell. He twisted around in the seat to look behind, to see in the unclear corner of his vision just once more the river, the silent, muddy Yalu. It was already far behind and dropping back more every minute, a languid trace of reflection among the hills and flatlands. He had never heard of it before he had come, and the closest he had been to it was a distance to be measured in vertical miles, but he felt that he knew it as well as a familiar street—its mud flats and wide mouth, its bridges, cities, bare banks, islands, and the lonely way it came from the interior. It seemed unbelievable that he would never see it again.

Almost from the moment that he parked his ship after landing, he began to experience a feeling of increasing detachment from the whole thing, of no longer being a participant or in any way involved in the war. It took an effort to draw himself back into it. He had no victories, only a hundred missions and a few Air Medals that had been awarded to him with all the objective deliberation of birthday presents. Now it was over. He wanted to be away as quickly as possible, to start forgetting.

There was a wait for orders that would send him home, however. They did not come immediately, and a week of complete idleness for him began. He tried to indulge in it. He stayed up and drank until the club closed at night, singing and telling stories. In the mornings, he slept late and spent the rest of the day out in the sun getting brown. Somehow, there was little pleasure in it. He was living by the wrong clock. Regularly, through the day, the doors would slam, the men wander out, and the trucks gun down to briefing. It was no privilege to lie in the warm sun and see them go, only a reminder of his passing as a comrade. Sometimes, he went to the ridge that ran behind the barracks and watched the fierce, hunting groups devour the runway and vanish to the north.

On the day of his departure, he stood with Cleve on the top of the hill and looked out across the field. His bags were gathered nearby, and they waited for the jeep that was to take him to the airport in Seoul. They would be able to see it coming for a full mile, down the straight run of road from the operations buildings, around the curve, and up the hill, throwing dust behind it all the way. It was a calm, sunny afternoon. A thin surf of heat waves washed across the runway, collapsing it before their eyes.

Speech seemed completely inadequate to Cleve. It transmitted nothing of time gone and ways dividing. He wanted to put his arm around DeLeo's shoulder.

"There seems to be a lot I haven't had a chance to say, Bert."

"That's right. All of a sudden."

"I think you know most of it, though."

DeLeo did not reply. He brushed a fly from his cheek.

"Remember that day when I first came into the flight? You were all sitting around the table?"

"Sure."

"You called yourself a wop."

DeLeo nodded abstractly.

"You've made it into one of the finest words I know."

"I wish you were going with me, Cleve."

"I wish you weren't leaving. Somehow I'm still not prepared for that."

"We'd spend a few days in Tokyo."

"Like the old times, eh?" He thought of it, everything passing swiftly and inconsecutively through his mind. On a morning long ago they had left to go there. "Well, I'll get to Tokyo. A little behind you this time."

"What do you have, twenty-one left?"

"Yes."

"That's not many."

"No. Enough maybe, but not many."

"It won't be long," DeLeo said.

The jeep was coming down the road. They both saw it, far off, and stood watching it approach. After a while they could hear the slamming of its axles on the rough surface and then the ripple of the engine. Cleve helped load the baggage in the rear seat. DeLeo sat down beside the driver. He reached out, and they shook hands with each other. It was the first time, Cleve felt certain, that they had ever done it.

"Take care of yourself, Cleve."

"You, too."

Their hands were still clasped, moving reflexively up and down.

"And good luck." The jeep began to move.

"So long," Cleve said.

DeLeo gave a little half-salute.

"*Sayonara*, Cleve."

He watched the jeep go up the road, make a quick turn, and start back down the hill, round the curve at the bottom, and travel along the road that paralleled the runway, a trail of thin, ascending dust behind it. Then it passed beyond the warehouses and out of sight. All along the road the soft film of dust still hung in the air. He turned and walked toward the barracks.

Being in a squadron was a digest of life. You were a child when you joined. There was endless opportunity, and everything was new. Gradually, almost unknowingly, the days of painful learning and delight were over; you achieved maturity; and then suddenly you were old, with new faces and relationships that were difficult to recognize rising up quickly all around you, until you found yourself existing practically unwelcome in the midst of them, with all the men you had known and lived with gone and the war little more than unsharable memories of things that had taken place long ago. It was like the last year of college, and the final examinations just over. Everybody was rushing to leave, many of them friends. Most of them you would never see again. Desmond was gone, Robey, Daughters, and DeLeo. The rooms were being continually filled with strangers, more of them every week. They knew nothing of the past and its holiness. For them, the war began the day of their arrival, and it would be a long time before they were tired of it and going home themselves, those that finished. Cleve searched, but he could not find himself among them. They were all so inexperienced and confident.

Two of them, replacements just assigned to his flight, came up to him in operations the next day and introduced themselves. They were like grandchildren, generations away from him.

"Kiser, sir," the first one said.

"Schramm."

"How much jet time do you have?" Cleve asked.

"Two hundred and twenty hours," Kiser said.

"I have about the same, two hundred and thirty-eight," the other added.

"Have you flown this airplane?"

"Yes, sir. In gunnery."

"That's good. How much time do you have in it?"

"Let's see. About forty hours, isn't that right?"

The second one nodded.

"How long will it be before we go on missions, Captain?" he asked.

"Well, there's a transition course you have to go through here. Three or four rides, normally."

"That's what we heard."

"Sometimes it takes a while to get the rides in," Cleve warned.

"Lieutenant Pell said it wouldn't be more than a couple of days."

It was that all the time now. Everybody knew him. As they passed him in the evenings or at noon, they would interrupt their conversation. They would turn to see him, to say something. The greetings followed him like wet grass clinging to footfalls in a meadow.

"Hey, Doctor," they said.

"Hello, Doc, Pell, buddy. Hi there! How's it going? Hello!"

Hunter and Pettibone were more and more with him. They echoed him when they talked. They appropriated fragments of his speech. It was like some law of the jungle. When he entered, they were behind. When he left, they followed. They gathered to him to protect themselves from oblivion and perhaps discover how to be blessed also. Whether with the innocence of children or in full understanding of what they were accepting, they were his undoubted disciples. With a cigar tucked in the corner of his mouth and looking like a boy imitating his father, Pell would give them advice.

"The most important thing now, Billy Lee, is to build up a lot of flying time—and to get promoted."

"I don't see how there's any chance of promotion," Hunter argued. They had all become first lieutenants less than a week previously.

"There isn't. That's why it's so important."

"I don't see how it's possible, though."

"There's always an angle," Pell said. "You ought to know that by now."

"I suppose so."

Cleve was alone. That was the life he almost seemed to have chosen. The time had gone by when it was easy to make friends. He walked by himself, the web of the past on him like a tangle of invisible rigging.

You lived and died alone, especially in fighters. Fighters. Somehow, despite everything, that word had not become sterile. You slipped into the hollow cockpit and strapped and plugged yourself into the machine. The canopy ground shut and sealed you off. Your oxygen, your very breath, you carried with you into the chilled vacuum, in a steel bottle. If you wanted to speak, you used the radio. You were as isolated as a deep-sea diver, only you went up, into nothing, instead of down. You were accompanied. They flew with you in heraldic patterns and fought alongside you, sometimes skillfully, always at least two ships together, but they were really of no help. You were alone. At the end, there was no one you could touch. You could call out to them, as he had heard someone call out one day going down, a pitiful, pleading "Oh, Jesus!" but they could touch you not.

He wrote to Eiko:

> *. . . the days seem really long. It feels like the hours aren't going anywhere except away, to some gathering place of all lost time, and slowly, very slowly. The air battles are irregular. They come in streaks. Many days with nothing and suddenly MIGs appear and it's a frenzy. It's hard to describe. You or them, suddenly, and everything counts.*

It was not all he wanted to say, but he was anxious to remind her that he was at the front, alone, as it were, defiant.

Heat and endless days. He leaned back in the chair and closed his eyes. He could not decide. Was it courage or enthusiasm, or something even more vital, life itself, that was draining out of him so steadily, day after day, mission after mission, as if a man were born with, or acquired, only so much of it, never to be replenished?

22

The days became hot buzzing. Long, dusty walks crossed them. Shoes scuffed at the dry earth, and the sun shone down heavy as mist. Voices at night carried far through the swollen air, and the weak glow of electric lights lasted late in the rooms. It was not easy to sleep—not like the winter with its hushed, blanketed hours and the metal of the stove creaking from the heat. The insects were bad, and there was only Korean ice.

Picking his missions carefully because he had so few remaining, Cleve went on. He chose only those that he calculated or guessed might be fruitful, deciding often at the last minute, trusting what was now a hardened, various instinct. There were not many fights, though. The failures added to each other, one by one. He went back over them frequently, all the opportunities lost. How many times had he chased after them when they were already above him, their bellies silver, sailing steadily away. Or gone down low to try and catch them climbing after takeoff, using up all his fuel in a gamble, so that when they did come from somewhere at the very end he could not stay and fight. Or doubled his bets, like a man at a roulette table, by compounding fruitless missions, one after the other, with the certainty that averages would finally work in his favor; but they did not. Or not seen them soon enough when they were there, and missed the critical moment that never returned. He thought of the next chance, if there was to be one, and alternated between bitter hope and despair. The nearly stagnant stream of days moved by.

On his eighty-fifth mission he went only because it was going far north and inland, away from the friendly water. He took it to discipline himself.

The day was cloudy; and they flew a long way past Huichon, in an unfamiliar northeasterly direction, to a junction where the fighter-bombers were hitting bridges across a river that the railroad followed. There was a level deck of clouds at twelve thousand feet. When they dropped down through it, it was like going beneath the surface of the sea. Everything in that submerged world was dim, cool, and unreal. The rugged hills were smothered with greenery like velvet, and the sagging roof of clouds close above made it like being in a great translucent cave. It was a place where he felt he could almost hear the sound of MIGs if they came, but they never did.

The time passed slowly. Every morning early and in the sweaty stillness of every night, he struggled with himself, stemming the weakness that seemed to come then. Open-eyed on his cot, he suffered through the darkness. Then, more than at any other time, there was the constant feeling that he was being consumed, drained; and he did not know the extent of his reserves. It was like flying with the fuel gauge reading zero, waiting for the silence that hit like a hammer. In the air, he did not lack aggressiveness. His determination was never missing there, but during the enormous hours in between he felt himself adrift and helpless. The fifteen, fourteen, thirteen missions ahead seemed many times more dangerous than those that had gone before, when he thought about them, which was often; and yet he simultaneously wished that he had back every one that had been wasted. He drove himself doggedly on.

Pell, by direction of Colonel Imil, was always leading an element, at least, on the missions.

"I want him in a firing position," the colonel said, not to Cleve. It had come down through the squadron commander and Nolan. "Leading flights if possible. I don't care if you have to put captains or even majors on his wing. He gets kills I want him out in front."

"He doesn't have very much experience, Colonel."

"To hell with the experience. I've got men with all the experience in the world and still not worth a damn."

"Yes, sir."

"Fly him in the lead from now on."

"Yes, sir."

Hunter and Pettibone both flew as his wingman. They were not especially happy to do it, but they didn't complain. Pell found MIGs, or, if he did not, they found him.

"I'm going to get one before I leave," Hunter said. "I don't care how. It doesn't matter whose wing I'm on. Just so I get my chance."

"He'll do all the shooting, though," Pettibone said.

"Not all of it. He's hot, that's the important thing. He's running into them all the time."

It was true. There seemed to be a fight only when Pell was in the air. For Cleve, there was an inevitability of the ships returning in twos, their noses blackened, their tanks gone, if the mission was one on which Pell went and he did not.

There was an escort for a photo-reconnaissance ship, and Pell filled in with another flight. He was leading the element in the close-cover group. Suddenly, there was a MIG nobody had seen coming in to make a pass on the photo ship. It leveled out right in front of Pell, not a thousand feet away. His sixth kill. When he taxied back in and parked that day, Colonel Imil jumped up on the wing of his ship and swore, impulsively, to get him the Distinguished Service Cross.

It was phenomenal. He was a wonder, a growing myth. He was, at that time, the most famous pilot in the Air Force, and it had all been accomplished in only fifty-odd missions. The bulk of his tour was still ahead of him. Letters containing clippings and photographs from newspapers in the States came almost daily. He read them and then filed them carefully away in cigar boxes. There was always something in the mail for him. Stamp collectors wrote, enclosing printed covers, and requested that he carry them to the Yalu and then endorse them back. Girls in cities he had never been to wrote, some sending their pictures. A periodical wanted an autobiography or at least an article. The president of an aircraft company sent congratulations.

They were already talking about who would get the flight when Cleve was gone. He had only eleven missions left. It would be soon.

"There isn't but one man in this group who can take over," Hunter announced.

Kiser was interested.

"Who's that?" he asked.

"Why, it's obvious."

"Pell?"

"Sure. See if he doesn't."

"Do you really think he'll get it?"

"He has to."

Kiser whistled.

"That's something. He was a brand-new second lieutenant when he came over, wasn't he?"

"A lot's happened since then."

"But don't they usually pick captains?"

"Not over a man with six kills."

"Say," Kiser asked, "were you with him on any? Did you see them?"

"Sure."

"What was it like?"

"Just like the combat film they show you."

"Yes," Kiser insisted, "but how did it start? How did he actually get them?"

"All kinds of ways," Hunter said. He was uncomfortable at having spoken too quickly. "Look, you'll see kills yourself; I guarantee you that."

There was a pause.

"Have you gotten any?"

"Not yet," Hunter said.

"I hope I'm along when you do."

"Maybe you will be."

Schramm came over and sat down with them. He was a quieter, more threatening fellow than Kiser.

"Has Cleve had the flight all along?" he said.

"Ever since the beginning. He's been here a long time."

"Since before Pell got here?"

"Oh, sure."

"How is it that he only has one MIG, then? Isn't he any good?"

"It's not that," Hunter said.

"How do you explain it then?"

"I don't know. He's old, for one thing."

"How old?"

"Thirty-five, maybe."

"He's a regular grandfather, isn't he?"

"He's a good pilot," Hunter said, moved by conscience. "You'd be better off with him than with anybody else, except you probably wouldn't find anything."

"Why?"

"I don't know. I just know that the Doctor is the one who gets them, and that's what counts. He's right in the thick of it every time. Once his leader got shot down right alongside of him, but he made it back."

"Is that right?"

"And got two MIGs while he was at it."

"What a mission that must have been," Kiser said.

"Yes, sir. I wasn't on that one, myself. If Pell doesn't get himself killed, though, he'll wind up top ace of the war. Mark my words. I've seen them come and go."

"You really think he'll get the flight?" Kiser said. "That would be something."

"He'd be a mean one to try and beat. He's a smart operator. Wait until you get to know him some."

"He looks mean," Schramm said. "I notice he's smoking on those cigars all the time."

"All fighter pilots smoke cigars," Hunter said.

23

In June came ponderous heat and mornings like eggshells, pale and smooth. Perhaps there might be a bit of early wind, warm but tantalizing, that was never repeated throughout the day. The heat was tremendous. It made the feet ache and clothes feel like abrasive. Even sheets were hot, concrete floors and water pipes. There was no place to go to escape it. The days were interminable. But the mornings, the eternal mornings! They were dawns of doomsday, already burned to transparence while still beyond the horizons over which they came. The mind was threatened by their emptiness. The face wrinkled instinctively against them. They were silent, like the dawns over vast sleeping millions, perfectly still, threatening, deathful. In their silence, premonitions bred like vermin, while red as a tomato the sun rose from behind the eastern hills, throwing down thick blankets of heat.

It was on such a morning that the first-light reconnaissance, which flew along the Chinese border visually checking the enemy fields, returned to report an awesome display. The strips were jammed with aircraft, a rash of silver MIGs strewn as thickly as pebbles on a shore. They had counted almost seven hundred of them, parked wingtip to wingtip.

"I knew it," Colonel Imil affirmed. The news reached him at breakfast. "I knew it."

"What's up?" Moncavage asked.

"They saw seven hundred MIGs up north this morning."

"Holy fish! What's going on?"

"They're loading up. They've been tipped off somehow."

"Tipped off to what?"

"I'll tell you later. Let's get down to the line."

They hurried off to combat operations, firing volleys of conversation at each other in the jeep. When they arrived, Moncavage knew.

"Only the best people today," Imil was saying as they strode in.

"All right."

"I want the cream of the group. This is the one, Monk. I can feel it. Seven hundred of them, by God! They're going to fight."

He was on the telephone direct to Fifth Air Force minutes later. It was not a good connection. His shouting into the mouthpiece could be heard all through the building.

"Listen, this is Imil. Our visual reccy flight just landed. What? Visual reccy. Yes, it just got back. They counted seven hundred MIGs up there. That's right. Yes. You goddamn well better. No, it's not here yet. Well, we'll be looking for it. Sure, sure, you bet. Sure."

He hung up and sat there, looking at Moncavage.

"Seven-thirty," he announced, consulting his watch. "They say the ops order will be here within two hours. A special courier is bringing it."

Moncavage puffed at a cigarette.

"Maybe I'd better start calling the squadrons."

"No," Imil said, "not yet. Don't get them keyed up. There's plenty of time."

"Do you want to wait in my office?"

"Let's wait right here. I want to open that envelope myself."

By eight, the pilots in the mess were talking about it. A fever mounted on the field, ominously, like lead melting. There were clusters of men everywhere discussing it—in the latrines, along the road, and out on the line. Something big was coming up. The level of excitement was rising like flood waters. All missions had been called off until further notice. Nobody knew more than that for certain.

At 1130 Hunter came bursting into the room. He looked about quickly.

"Where's Cleve?"

"What have you heard?" Pell said.

"They want everybody down in the briefing room in fifteen minutes. The whole group."

"Even the new sports?" He nodded toward Kiser and Schramm.

"Everybody, they said."

"Do you know what it is yet?"

"No," Hunter said. "Where's Cleve?"

"Who cares?" Pell stood up. "Let's go, men. You, too, Petti."

Hunter stayed behind. He ran from room to room. They were empty. Everybody had gone. After what seemed like ten minutes, he located Cleve sunning himself behind the barracks. There was another wait while Cleve got dressed. It was a quarter to twelve before they left for operations. All the vehicles had gone already. They had to walk.

They arrived ten minutes late. The whole group was already there. The briefing room overflowed. There were not enough seats for all of them; pilots were standing up in the back of the room. Colonel Moncavage was prowling the center aisle checking for complete attendance. He looked toward them as they entered.

"Thanks for coming, Connell," he said. Heads turned.

The room was baking hot. As the minutes dragged by, restlessness grew. There were coughs and the sound of matches being struck. Thickening smoke made the air even more unbreathable. At 1215 the colonels were still talking earnestly to each other in the front of the room. Cleve stood looking through the blue haze at the map forty feet away. He squinted his eyes but could not make out anything written on it. The schedule board, too, was blank. Nothing was up there except the familiar, laconic sign at top center of the wall: The Fighting Heart. With posed, disinterested expressions the pilots waited. Finally, Colonel Imil stood up and walked toward the low platform. He stepped up onto it.

"Well, boys," he said. It became perfectly silent. "This is the one we've all been waiting for. This should be the biggest one of the war."

He paused. Cleve could feel his heart beginning to pound. His thoughts leaped sickeningly. The biggest one. A strike against Antung. The fields north of the Yalu. That was the first thing that came to him.

"The joint chiefs in Washington," Imil continued, "have finally given the green light. Today, we're going after the dam at Sui Ho."

There was a hum of recognition. The target was on the Yalu itself.

"That's the fourth biggest one in the world, with the second greatest output of power," Imil said. "We haven't touched it up until now. Too hot, I suppose; but it's finally been approved. Every fighter-bomber in Fifth Air Force is going up there today, right across the river from the MIGs. They'll be able to see the smoke from their fields, and they'll be coming up, too, all of them, to stop us. You can count on that. I don't have to tell you who'll be leading them, either. You know as well as I do. He'll be there. You can bet your life on it. Our job is to get those fighter-bombers in and out, and that's what we're going to do. Every ship that can fly is going. Do you have the numbers from the squadrons yet, Monk?"

"Right here."

"Read them off."

Moncavage announced the totals for each squadron: twenty-two planes, eighteen, and twenty. He gave a list to one of the operations officers who copied it onto the scheduling board, number by number. Then each squadron supplied the names of the pilots who would go, and they, too, were written down. Cleve watched as the eighteen blanks for his squadron were filled. The squadron commander was leading the first flight, with Pell and Pettibone as his element. Gabriel and three from that flight were next; then the operations officer, Nolan, and three from his old flight. At the very bottom, posted beside the two ships that made up the odd element, Connell and Hunter. It took only a few minutes until the list for the entire group was complete. The takeoff times were being written in.

"All right," Imil said. "Weather."

Cleve listened lightly. The words went skimming across his consciousness. He could feel his palms sweating.

". . . scattered cumulus," the weather officer was saying, "with bases at about two thousand and tops five to six thousand. There may be occasional buildups higher than that late in the afternoon. At thirty-five thousand a thin deck of cirrus, nothing more than scattered. Visibility throughout the area, fifteen miles or better."

He went on to give the winds aloft, the azimuth and elevation of the sun, the condition of the tides, temperatures of the air and water, and finally the runway in use at the time of takeoff.

"What about contrails?" Imil asked.

"I don't think you'll see cons today at any altitude."

"Good," Imil said. "Now here's the way we'll go in."

He began outlining takeoff times for the flights and squadrons, then the patrol altitudes. He told which of the fighter-bomber groups were going in first, and from what direction. He warned of the many guns, heavy and light, in the target area. They were all marked on the wall behind him.

Cleve jotted notes down on his map. He and Hunter would be the last ones off. That didn't surprise him. He could feel warm beads running heavily down his back in the hollow between the shoulders and down his calves. It was unbearably hot in the room. They had been there for at least thirty minutes.

"Boys," Imil was saying, "I kid you not. They'll be up there today. I wouldn't be surprised if there were five hundred of them. And they're going to be after those fighter-bombers down below us. Fine, I say. We'll be waiting for them.

"You flight leaders! Be aggressive. Don't waste your time on long shots. Get in close where you won't miss. And element leaders. I want you covering the flight leader as long as you can. Split up when you have to and not before. You wingmen. You've got the toughest job of all. Keep your eyes open. Keep your leader cleared. The air is going to be loaded with ships today, so don't be calling a break for some goddamned speck five miles behind you. Make sure that they're MIGs and that it's time to break. Everybody! Keep off the radio unless you've got something important to say. Don't clutter up the air with long conversations. If you lose each other up there, go to another channel and work it out. Watch your fuel. Don't stay up there until you're down to just barely enough to make it home, because if you do and you get bounced on the way back, you'll never get there. When you're down to fifteen hundred pounds today, clear out. Don't make that one last sweep. Get going right then.

"This is one time when there'll be MIGs enough for everybody. When you see them, go after them; and when you get close, put that pipper on them and keep it there. Hold down that trigger as long as you're hitting them. I don't want to hear about any goddamned damages when we come back. I want to hear about kills. Nothing but kills. Remember that." He paused. "You can take a look around you right now, because there'll probably be some empty seats here tomorrow. Just make sure it isn't you.

"All right. Let's get them!"

They were all on their feet and standing in place while the colonel stepped down from the platform and made his way between them toward the door at the rear of the room. Then came a general foot-shuffling movement as the pilots followed him out, jamming up at the door and waiting until they could funnel through. Cleve stood in the midst of them, carried along by the flow. He glanced at Hunter, who smiled cheerlessly. For some reason that defied isolation, Cleve had the feeling that he had flown this mission already, once before in days long past, and was now about to do it again.

"Feeling lucky, Gabe?" Imil said. He was out in the debriefing room calling to individuals in the crowd moving past him.

Gabriel nodded unthinkingly.

"How about you, Doctor? Are you going to get them?"

"You bet," Pell said. He held up his small fist.

"That's the way," Imil grinned.

He stood there, looking staunch for everybody. He was full of excitement and nervousness himself. Occasionally, he clapped his hand on a passing shoulder.

"This is the one, boy," he would say.

He turned once, abruptly, and feinted as if to punch Moncavage in the stomach. He laughed.

"What do you say, Monk?"

"I'm ready," Moncavage said, after having to clear his throat.

"So am I. So am I."

The locker room was stuffy and filled with flies. It was too early to dress. Cleve had more than an hour to wait. He went outside with Hunter and sat on a bench partially shaded by one of the eaves. It was quiet there. They sat aimlessly, soundless drums beating within them.

"The last damned flight," Hunter said. "What a place to be on a mission like this. It'll all be over by the time we get there."

Cleve did not reply.

"One of your last missions and all, too. I think it's pretty rotten."

"So do I."

"I wish you'd said something."

"Who to? The chaplain?"

"One of the colonels," Hunter said. "The major. Anybody."

Cleve laughed.

"That's it," he said, "the true comic touch. I'd be better off praying."

"You oughtn't to joke about that. I've prayed here more than once."

"How'd you make out?"

"I mean it."

"Well, I know. That's why I asked."

"They haven't been answered yet," Hunter said truthfully. "They will be, though."

"It's always a possibility, I guess."

Not much later, almost unexpectedly, there was the sound of the first ships starting their engines. Cleve looked toward it. The black ramp seemed to be melting in the heat. Upon it, like mirages, stood the baking aircraft. He could see the wash of curdled air that was the jet exhaust billowing up behind the starting ships. He walked inside with Hunter and dressed slowly.

He was bathed in sweat when he carried his equipment out to the ship. The sun lay on his shoulders and back with a weight almost equal to that of the parachute. He felt thirsty. His mouth and throat were dry.

They were still working on something on his airplane. He laid his things on the left wing and walked around to the nose to see what was being done. The armament man was having some trouble. A defective magazine had become jammed in the gun camera, and he could not remove it.

"It's stuck halfway in there," he explained. "I can't get it in or out either one now."

"Let me try," Cleve said.

He reached into the narrow opening with his own hand and tried to force the film package to move. His fingers were slippery, and in the confined space a good purchase was difficult. He could not move it either.

"It's all right," he said. "Leave it as it is. You can work on it when I get back."

"Yes, sir."

He walked around the airplane, inspecting it, and then climbed into the cockpit and began strapping himself in. This occupied him for a while. When he was finished, he looked at his watch. Still several minutes remaining. He felt he had been waiting for hours. His thirst was very strong by now, and he seemed to be sitting in a pool of searing air. Every piece of metal about him was too hot to touch. He could feel the sweat going down his legs in hesitating streams. Finally, it was time. He started his engine.

It was even hotter taxiing out, but by that time a kind of transition had been completed. He was immersed in discomfort. He no longer noticed it. It was even satisfying to be so baptized. The interior of his oxygen mask was as slippery as fish, and the air he drew from it was warm and flatulent, but at last he was fully involved in the mission and far beyond any of the trivialities that went with it.

As he taxied through them, pools of soft tar at the end of the runway sucked at his wheels and splattered up in oversized drops to stain the underside of the wings. He lined up and waited until Hunter drew alongside him. They ran up their engines. He looked across. Hunter nodded. Cleve dropped his raised right hand, and simultaneously they released their brakes. Gathering speed, they moved down the runway together. It was the highest moment of confidence forever renewed upon taking off, the soaring of spirit. Cleve felt light and new again, invincible. They were moments of well-being that did not last long. They were gradually replaced by nervousness. Cleve could feel it running through him, as they started north.

24

Flashing like fish silver, they broke through a low, billowing surf of clouds and into unmarked sky. They climbed. They crossed the Han and into enemy territory, passing the invisible line beyond which little was forgiven. Time seemed to be going quickly. The tempo of landmarks was greater than usual. The compounding hands of the altimeter seemed to be moving more rapidly. Over the radio, nothing except for routine traffic. The fight had not started. Cleve felt elated. He had not hoped for such luck.

He looked back toward Hunter, and his courage and pride swelled. There was nothing to compare with the happiness of leading. Toward the final test and winnowing they flew together, and though a man on the ground could neither see nor hear them, they were up, specks of metal moving through a prehistoric sky, contaminating an ocean of air with only their presence, electrifying the heavens. Cleve felt a distilled fulfillment. For these moments, no price could be too high.

As they neared the Yalu, the cloudiness increased, and above a spotty floor of white there was one huge cumulus buildup, a towering mushroom of brightness as big as a county. It looked like a cosmic fungus, like layers of wrath. They were at forty thousand feet then and climbing. The river was still five minutes away.

Suddenly, cutting through the lesser voices, there was Colonel Imil's.

"Dust on the runway at Antung, boys," he called. "Heads up."

It was as if they had waited for him, Cleve thought slowly. He tried to see the reddish plumes rising, but the cumulus was in the way. Beyond that vast cloud and beneath it, they were taking off to fight. He began searching the sky with the intensity of a man who has lost a diamond on a public beach.

The first train was called out, a confirmation of the colonel's sighting. Less than a minute later, they were announcing a second. Then a third.

"They're climbing to altitude north of the river," Imil said. "It won't be long."

As Cleve reached the river, they were up to five bandit trains. He turned northeast, toward the dam and reservoir already marked by noiseless explosions that seemed as small as those made by stones dropped into lake silt. He watched as they appeared irregularly in unexpected places. Smoke from a big fire was starting to rise. He looked behind. Hunter was in good position, steady as a shadow. Over the radio an unemotional voice was tolling again:

"Bandit trains numbers six and seven leaving Antung, heading north. Trains six and seven leaving Antung."

He reached the reservoir and turned back toward the southwest, high, higher than the others, climbing very gradually all the time. There was a brittle expectancy running through the flights. Urgent, confused calls came continually over the radio, but nobody had made definite contact. Nobody was in a fight yet. The eighth and ninth trains were announced. It would all happen at once. He felt himself living by individual seconds. He flew along the river, turning at the mouth.

"Bandit train number ten is on a heading of three three zero. Train number ten heading three three zero."

Ten was more than he remembered ever having heard. The eleventh was called, and twelve, like compartments filling in a stricken ship. It was a flood. Strangely, he could feel the skin all over his shoulders and back, as if there were eyes staring at it. His sensitivity was almost unbearable. Then he heard Hunter's quick voice:

"Bogies high at ten o'clock!"

He looked up into the vacant sky to his left.

"Five, six of them," Hunter called.

Six. That number made it a certainty. Cleve started a gentle turn to the left, trying to locate them as he did.

"I don't have them."

"They're at ten o'clock, high, way out, passing to nine now!"

Cleve looked. The sky was bright, empty blue. He stared hard at it, fighting to see, working painfully across it.

"Do you have them?" Hunter cried anxiously.

Surely they would appear at any second. The effort made his eyes water.

"No," he said at last. "I don't have them. Go ahead, you take them."

Hunter did not turn. Cleve watched him and waited.

"Go ahead. Take them."

There was still a pause.

"Aw," Hunter said, "I've lost them now."

In silence they took up a track along the river again. The last of the fighter-bombers were going in toward the dam, serenely, but he knew how they must feel. Everybody was uneasy. It was unbelievable that the MIGs would not strike, but slowly, as the minutes sank away, he began to accept it. Flights were starting to leave the area, low on fuel. He heard Imil turning toward home. He checked his own gauge: twenty-one hundred pounds.

They were going up the river, throttled back now for economy and descending slightly all the while to maintain good speed. They reached the reservoir and flew about twenty miles past it before turning toward Antung again. Halfway there, he called Hunter.

"How much do you have, Billy?"

"Eighteen hundred pounds."

One more time, he thought. He listened impassively to more and more flights starting their withdrawals, intact, unsuccessful. In roughly the same order that they had arrived in, their fuel dropped to the minimum, and they departed. Fortune was a matter to be measured in minutes. At Antung, as he swung around toward the northeast, he had sixteen hundred pounds.

"Just once more," he said. "How much do you have now?"

"Fifteen hundred."

They started up the river. It was like swimming alone far out to sea. The minutes were a tide they were moving against. His eyes kept coming back to the fuel gauge. He knew it would be motionless for as long as he could look at it, like a clock. Finally, they were at the reservoir. The radio was almost silent. They were among the last ones remaining within fifty miles. They made a large orbit to the left and encountered nothing. They had stayed too long. Turning south, Cleve had twelve hundred pounds. He started climbing for home.

He looked in Hunter's direction, back, over his shoulder. A memorial smoke hung over Sui Ho. He stared for a few moments. On the other side, as he turned his head, the great cumulus still rose near Antung, but now it seemed as inanimate and fading as an extinct volcano. It was a relic, enormous in a lonely sky. His gaze moved slightly. Something that could not be seen had drawn it, a force beyond all things sensory. He continued to watch idly, without a motive. Then, as if from out of nothing, so far off and delicate that if he were to move his eyes even slightly or blink he would not be able to pick them up again, airplanes appeared. He could not glance into the cockpit to check his fuel. He called Hunter instead, as he began turning toward them.

"How much fuel, Green Two?"

"I'm down to eleven hundred. What are you turning north again for?"

Cleve did not answer. He maintained his focus. The ships slowly grew to be unmistakable specks. They were still miles away, becoming not so much bigger as slightly darker. A minute later, Hunter called them out.

"Four bogies off at one o'clock, Lead!"

"I have them."

"They're crossing to two now. They're starting in!"

"What?" Cleve said. The ships he was looking at were no more than decimal points.

"Four of them coming down from three o'clock, Cleve!"

Then, "Get ready to break!"

He looked quickly up to his right. There were MIGs, four of them. He had not even seen them, concentrating as he had been on the ones out ahead.

"Take it around to the right, Billy!"

They turned into the attacking ships. The MIGs did not continue in, then, but pulled back up. Cleve watched them flash overhead. He reversed his turn to follow. He watched with chilling recognition as they did something he had never seen before. They split into pairs.

"We've got some cool ones this time, Billy."

"Cleve?"

"Roger."

"Did you get a good look at them?"

"Yes. Why?"

"The leader has black stripes."

His heart became audible. Something opened within him, full and frightening. He watched them as they swung apart, trying to pick the one out. Of all the times to have his chance. He came close to laughing, but he was too electrified.

"Are you sure?"

"Absolutely."

Yes, absolutely. To finally meet him, this far north with this much fuel. He looked at his gauge now: nine hundred pounds. He could almost feel the tanks draining as he flew. It was like blood from his own arteries.

"Let's keep working south," he said.

They were not to do it that easily, though. The MIGs started back in, working in coordinated pairs: two first, with two more timing their pass so that they would be coming in behind Cleve as he met the others. It took skill to operate that way. It was difficult, and murderous if expertly done. He waited as long as he could before turning into the nearest ones. He wanted to carry the fight as far south as possible. The MIGs might be low on fuel, too.

"Around to the left," he said.

The first two were already in close. He strained to watch them over his shoulder, the Gs tugging at his head. They were firing. The cannon tracers were streaming by, just behind and below him, like dashes of molten ore.

They did not follow in the turn, but began climbing right back up, to achieve position and come in again. The two teams of them were going to work like that. As the MIGs went by behind him the first time, he called, "Reverse it!" to Hunter, hoping to get a shot in as they went away from him. He was not able to. He was behind them, but too far back and out of line. He stole a glance over his shoulder. He could not see Hunter.

"You with me, Billy?"

There was no answer.

"Billy!"

"I'm all right."

Cleve looked back again, on both sides. He still could not see him.

"Break right!" he heard Hunter call.

It was the second pair. Cleve turned into them as hard as he could. He caught sight of Hunter then a little below him, turning too. The MIGs fired and passed behind him. Cleve rolled out of the turn immediately. He was heading west. He turned back toward the south. As he did, he saw the first two coming in again, but not from so good a position this time. They were too far forward. Cleve was going to be able to meet them almost head on. He turned into them and, at the last second, was able to fire as they came. Hunter was firing, too.

They passed the MIGs in a brief instant, and Cleve turned hard after them, without hesitation, caught up in the blood lust, brimming with lunacy. He was fighting for any advantage, and the MIGs were not climbing away. They were turning, too. He was astonished to see it. He recognized the chance.

He was not completely conscious of what he was doing or even planning. A hand that had done this for years was guiding his ship. He was merely riding along, it seemed, striving to see better, to see everything; and he was cutting the MIGs off slightly in the turn, getting inside them. He could distinguish the black markings on the leader. He pulled after him, distended. As he did, still far from being in a position to shoot, he was stricken with a sense of resignation and fear. They went around and around in this silent, unyielding circle. His fuel was getting lower and lower. He glanced quickly at it: seven hundred pounds. They were going down steadily; they had passed through twenty thousand. The airspeed was building. He had lost sight of the other two MIGs, of Hunter, of everything but the winding earth and the lead ship turning with him, motionless as the world spun about them.

They were passing fourteen thousand. They might go all the way, to the deck. Every minute made fuel more critical, and at full throttle in the lower altitudes they were using it prodigiously. It was a devouring circle. He could not break out of it without being in a worse position in a running fight if they followed him, but he did not have fuel enough to continue, either. He needed every remaining pound just to get back.

"You st . . . have me, Billy?" He spoke with difficulty. The words came out distorted by Gs.

"Roger. You're clear."

He could hear Hunter's breath over the radio, being forced out of him.

They kept turning, fighting for position. He was not gaining now. He was a quarter of the circle behind holding that spot, turning, turning, turning while the MIG held still ahead of him. They were struggling for the slightest change. The airplanes no longer seemed involved. It was a battle of wills, of the strength to hang on, as if by the teeth alone. To let up meant to lose, and it was Cleve's advantage. He was rigid with the determination to stay there.

Suddenly the MIG rolled over and started down. For an endless part of a second Cleve hesitated, surprised. They were very low. He was not sure he could follow him through and clear the ground. He was almost certain the MIG could not make it. He knew a moment of awful decision, and then rolled and followed. They were going straight down, in a split S, wide open. They burst through the level of clouds. The earth was shooting up at him. The stick seemed rigid. He trimmed and pulled back as hard as he could, popping the speed brakes to help pitch him through. Everything faded into gray and then black. When it began to be gray again, he saw that they had made it. He was right behind Casey, on the deck. The hills and trees were whipping past just beneath them. His ship slammed and jolted crazily against ripples of air.

Casey broke left. French curves of vapor trailed from his wingtips. Cleve was behind him, on the inside, turning as hard as he could. The bright pipper of his sight was creeping up on the MIG, jerkily, but moving slowly up to the tail, the fuselage, the wing root. He squeezed the trigger. The tracers arced out, falling mostly behind. There were a few strikes near the tail. He could hardly hold the wild pipper where it was, but somehow he moved it forward, it seemed only inches more.

They were just above the trees. He could not take his eyes off the MIG to look, but he saw from their corners an avalanche of green and brown flashing fatally by. He fired again. His heart ballooned into his throat. He shouted into the mask, not words, but a senseless cry. Solid strikes along the fuselage. There was a burst of white flame and a sudden flood of smoke. The MIG pulled up sharply, climbing. It was slipping away from him, but as it did, he laced it with hits. Finally, trailing a curtain of fire, it rolled over on one wing and started down.

"There he goes!"

Cleve could not answer.

"Head south," he finally said. "Do you have the other ones in sight?"

"Not now."

"All right. Let's go."

They turned for home, climbing, too low on fuel to make it, Cleve was certain. The other MIGs had vanished. They were alone in the sky. He checked his fuel: three hundred and fifty pounds.

"How much do you have?" he asked Hunter.

"Say again, Cleve."

"What state fuel?"

"I'm down to . . . down to three hundred now."

"We'll climb as high as we can."

The engines drank as they climbed. It was a hemorrhage. They were paying for altitude with an open-throated flow. It poured away. The needle of the gauge seemed to fail as Cleve looked at it. The minutes were endless. He suffered through them, trying not to think, restraining himself. He looked out to sea, where they would probably end up. It had always seemed a sanctuary. Now it was unnerving, a place to drown in. He thought of the bailing out. He had never left an airplane before, and the moment of abandoning that close cockpit for sheer, climactic space chilled him.

They were climbing fast. The ships performed better the emptier they became, and the blackfaced dial then showed just less than one hundred pounds. It was hardly enough to wet the bottom of the tank. They were past Sinanju, but with more than a hundred miles to go.

"What do you have now, Billy?"

"Not enough to mention."

"Empty?"

"Almost," Hunter said. "Do you think we'll make it?"

"Well," Cleve began. He was interrupted.

"Oh, oh! There it is," Hunter said.

"Did you run out?"

"Yes."

Cleve looked at his own gauge. It read zero, although the engine was still running. He shut it off. There could not be more than a minute or two of fuel left, anyway.

It was almost absolutely silent, gliding evenly together. They were at thirty-eight thousand feet. It was all up to the winds aloft and the exact number of miles remaining. He looked out ahead. They still had a long way to go. The altimeter unwound: thirty-seven thousand.

They glided south, descending steadily as the unyielding miles fell behind them. The altimeter surrendered feet mechanically: thirty-six thousand five hundred. Thirty-six thousand. He watched it creep and then hurry, like a nightmare's clock, as slowly, gently, they fell from grace. He listened to the valves in his mask open and close to his breathing. Thirty-five thousand. It all had to happen at the most regulated pace. The airspeed was important. A few knots too high or low meant miles. He guarded it carefully. Thirty-four thousand. Thirty-three thousand five hundred.

He reassessed the chances constantly, checking the altitude against his map. There were things that had to be guessed, but he computed over and over. Thirty-two thousand. The moment he dreaded was when he would have to decide between heading for the water or continuing toward the Han, trying to make it all the way. That was the final commitment. He kept waiting, hoping to be sure. Thirty-one thousand. Finally the time came.

He did not really have to choose. He continued south. Afraid or not, he had decided beforehand. The feeling in his stomach was heavy as mercury. Perhaps he had not decided really, but only failed to decide. It did not matter. The hand of the altimeter was moving a little faster.

At twenty-five thousand, with the field far off, not yet visible, he heard somebody calling. It was Imil, back at the base.

". . . now, Green Lead?"

"I can't read you. Say again."

"What's your position? Where are you now, Green Lead?"

"We're about forty miles north."

"How much fuel do you have?"

"None."

"What?"

"We're both empty."

There was a thoughtful silence.

"Do you have enough altitude to make it across the Han?"

"I think so," Cleve answered. "It's going to be close."

"Get out if you can't make the field. Don't ride it down."

"Understand."

"But try and make it."

They were passing through seventeen thousand. The air grew thicker all the way down, more viscous, so that they had to keep lowering the nose slightly to maintain speed. The ship felt heavier and heavier as it passed from the abstraction of deep air and slipped closer to the solid, irresistible ground. The field was in sight now. Fifteen thousand.

"Did you get any?" the colonel asked abruptly.

"Roger."

"How many?"

"One."

There was no reply.

At eleven thousand feet they were gliding across the mouth of the Han. The water bore the flat gleam of daylight. The backs of the hills were edged with shadows. In the cockpit with the engine dead, the silence was cruel as Cleve alternately abandoned and then retook hope. He altered course slightly to line up better with the runway. If they were able to reach the field they would have to land straight in.

"If it looks like we won't make it," Cleve said, "get out at two thousand feet. Don't wait any longer than that, Billy."

"Roger. I think we're going to be all right, though."

"Maybe."

Cleve was slightly in front. When he passed through eight thousand feet he was still not absolutely certain, but shortly after that he knew. He could make it. The last thousand feet, coming easily down the path of the final approach he knew so well, was overwhelmingly fulfilling. Dead sticking it in, he landed a little long but smoothly in the stillness. He felt an emptying relief as his wheels touched the runway. He cracked the canopy open. The fair wind came in to cool him.

Hunter misjudged. He had been off to one side and a little lower than Cleve, and when he saw that he was going to be short, he tried to stretch his glide, turning very low at the last with not enough speed left. There was that moment of immense awkwardness, as when a wall begins to fall outward into a crowd. He crashed just north of the field. There was no fire. It was a dry, rending disintegration that plowed up a storm of dust.

They towed Cleve's ship in from the end of the runway. Halfway back, Colonel Imil came driving up. He jumped onto the wing.

"Well, you made it, anyway," he said.

"Is Hunter all right?"

"They're out there now. I haven't heard."

"I thought he was going to make it," Cleve said.

"He was half a mile short. It wasn't even close."

In the parking area they were gathered, pilots and crewmen. They pressed close as the plane came to a stop. Cleve looked out at the rash of faces. He recognized some. Others were like those at a station, seen from a moving train. He could hear the armorers clearing his guns. The bolts clapped forward.

"How did it happen?" the colonel asked.

"We were jumped on the way back," Cleve said. They were all listening. He was conscious of that. They were stretching their necks to hear. "There were four of them, tough babies. They finally ran us out of fuel."

"You got one, though?"

He felt his heart skip and his hands become weightless from

what he was about to cast before them, to hold high like a severed head. One? He was not in complete control of himself. He could have laughed with tears running from his eyes. Had he gotten one? They were all packed close, looking up, the strong and the slight, the famous and the unfulfilled. He opened his mouth a little to prevent the words from forming there and bursting out. He knew how to say it, the phrase that stilled trumpets, that fell like a great tree; but he had to wait. He gazed out over their open faces.

Somebody was pushing through to the airplane. Cleve watched. He saw Pell just below, his hands in his hip pockets, his expression querulous. Somebody squeezed past Pell. It was Colonel Moncavage. He had come from the wreck.

"Is he all right?"

Moncavage was trying to get up on the wing.

"Is Hunter all right?"

Imil took his arm and pulled him up.

"He's dead," Moncavage said.

"Nice going," Pell's voice rose piercingly.

Cleve stepped slowly over the side of the ship down to the wing. Suddenly he was tired, not physically; his whole body was still quickened with what had been done and the accident of being alive, but he was tired of everything else.

"You got one of them, anyway," Imil said flatly.

"Yes."

Below, near the nose of the ship, there was an exclamation.

"The film didn't run, Colonel," somebody called.

The magazine was handed up. Imil turned it over, inspecting it. He scratched at the little green footage window with his thumbnail several times.

"Not a foot," he said, passing it to Moncavage. "There goes the damned confirmation."

"It doesn't matter," Cleve said.

"Don't be so goddamned casual. Of course it matters."

"Not this time."

"What are you talking about?" Imil asked sharply.

"It was Casey Jones."

There was a moment of catastrophic silence, and as Cleve watched, he knew it was one for which he would not be forgiven.

"Are you sure?"

Cleve nodded. He hardly heard the words. He was listening to the murmur that had started to run like wind through deep grass.

"Are you sure?" Imil repeated.

Pell interrupted.

"There's no film, Colonel," he cried.

"That's right," Imil said uncertainly. He looked at Moncavage, who shrugged.

"There's no one to confirm it now, either," Pell said.

"No," Imil agreed. He decided quickly. That was certain enough. "There's not."

Cleve looked at them, one by one. Nothing was real. He heard a short, insane cough of contempt leave his lips. He did not know what he was thinking, only that he was far removed, farther than he had ever believed possible.

"Oh yes, there is," he said blindly.

"Who?"

"I can confirm it." He drew a sudden breath. "Hunter got him."

It had come out almost subconsciously. Malice had brought it, and protest, and the sweeping magnanimity that accompanies triumph, but, as soon as he said the words, he realized there were no others that would have made it right.

Billy Hunter would have his day as a hero, and in memory be never less of a man than he had been on his last flight. Cleve could give him that, at least—a name of his own. It was strange. In all that had passed, he had never imagined anything faintly like it, to have searched the whole heavens for his destiny and godliness, and in the end to have found them on earth.

He had kept a pledge. His heart cried out to go among them and tell them how he had fulfilled whatever promise he had, how in the clean sky he had met and conquered a legend. He lay on his cot that night, the draining finally effective, unable to move. He was conscious of nothing except his weakness and surrender to a great fatigue. With his eyes closed to make a double darkness, he lay awake in the still summer night, victorious at last and feeling as little a desire to live as he had ever known.

25

At the close of June, he had only four missions left. A winter had gone by, a drowsy spring, and part of a summer. In time, the mornings would be cool again with another autumn. To Cleve it seemed as if years and not months had passed. His first days in Korea now were like the vague, distant ones of childhood, simple and carefree. It was hard to associate himself with them. His memory faltered as he tried to retreat to that time so long ago and served him only with unreal, overlapping scenes and conversations.

It was near the end for him, and, as if in its final throes, the terrible fever to win that had held him was stronger than it had ever been. He no longer suffered, though. He had endured it too long. It was a part of him, permanently burned in. He felt untroubled, not satisfied but insensitive at last. He had been cleansed.

Hunter was going to be awarded the Silver Star. Imil had promised that. With a solitary red star beside it, Hunter's name was listed on the claims board where he had always wanted it. That was not much, compared with Pell's galaxy, but it would have meant everything to Hunter. And Cleve was at lonely peace with himself. He felt as if he had finally passed from youth into a real maturity, one in which he soberly realized the price that had to be paid to abide by the ideals that were once so bright and compelling. The reckoning was dear; but for all that they had cost him, he held them even more fiercely. He had nothing frivolous remaining to believe in then, only an obdurate residue more precious than a handful of diamonds.

With Pettibone on his wing, he flew north on his ninety-seventh mission. There was not a cloud in the sky. They crossed the Haeju Peninsula and then the edge of an unblemished sea that lay like a sheet of foil in the sunlight, climbing again to those great heights where the mind was transmuted. A fight was developing. The MIGs were taking off from Antung. Somebody was describing the cloud of dust rising there. Cleve could hear the tempo of talk on the radio increasing, like a current as it nears rapids.

Free of the gravitational forces of reality, he sat in the sunshine and looked out over a crystal empire. Antung lay under a dome of clear air that reached every horizon. The river, its bridges, and the earthen town beside it were as small as a history book map. It was almost sleep-inducing. He knew a tranquillity as timeless as a dream of deepest waters. If death were ever to touch him here, it would be with a gesture of equality, with fingertips only. In this high, sterile realm he would fight and, conquering, it seemed, become immortal. He heard a flight dropping tanks. They had sighted MIGs crossing at the reservoir. His heart beat as wildly as ever while he listened. He would be there in a few minutes at the most. There was a joy unlike any he had known going north that day, penetrating farther and farther, north into Casey's country, into his own.

He was not disappointed. There was a big fight. High and low, in great numbers, the MIGs came streaming south. Every man who wanted to found them, and some who did not. Pell got his seventh.

The debriefing room was wild after they returned, with the first flushed men gathered at the tables and talking all at once. Others came through the door in twos and threes, their flying suits dark with sweat, their faces creased and dirty where the masks had been. They crowded to the tables, talking excitedly as they did, interrupting each other and pausing only briefly to listen.

The room was in sustained confusion. There was a flow of faces moving continually by, faces glistening, reflective, exuberant, dulled. Among them was Pell's, followed by that of a correspondent interviewing him on his seventh victory. They paused in the very center of the room. Pell continued giving the details, watching the tablet on which they were being scribbled, upside down. He paced himself by the man's pencil. There were long hesitations. During one, he could hear a voice behind him that was topping the steady surf of those in the room.

"We were separated right at the beginning. I wasn't able to pick him up again after the first time we broke. They were all over me from then on."

It was Pettibone. Pell turned around and saw him standing between the two colonels, looking from one to the other as he talked.

"Didn't you call him?"

"I called him half a dozen times."

"Well?"

"He never answered. I never heard anything. I called and called."

"All right," Colonel Imil said. "Where did it happen?"

They bent over the map as Pell pushed his way through to them and forced a space for himself at the table. Pettibone had trouble locating the spot. His finger wandered over the paper hesitantly as he tried to indicate where the fight had taken place. Finally he traced out an area about ten miles square. It was right on the Yalu.

"Somewhere along in here, I think," he said.

"Set up a couple of flights right away in case we have to cap him, Monk, and check around. Somebody else may have seen him."

Colonel Moncavage hurried off.

"What happened?" Pell asked. "Where's Connell?"

Pettibone looked up at him pleadingly.

"I don't know."

"You don't know?"

"I lost him in the fight, and he's not back yet."

They stood there, looking down at the map that covered the entire surface of the table.

"Right in here somewhere," Pettibone added, pointing again to the place.

After a few minutes, Colonel Moncavage was back with a pilot from one of the other squadrons who was able to tell them something more. He had been in that same area with his flight at the time. He remembered hearing Pettibone's calls. A little later he had seen Cleve's ship. One wing had been shot off it. He had watched it going down in a long, shallow trajectory near the river, spinning over and over like an elm pod all the way.

"Are you sure it was him?"

"I don't know who it was, Colonel."

"It was one of ours, though?"

"Yes, sir. The MIGs were still shooting at it."

"Did you see a parachute?"

"It looked like the canopy was still on the ship, the last I saw of it, Colonel."

There was a pensive silence.

"Then you didn't see it crash," Imil said at length.

"I couldn't even keep it in sight. We were right in the MIGs ourselves, then."

"Well," the colonel said, "I guess that's it."

He drummed his fingers on the table as he thought about it. Then he turned and walked out of the room toward the switchboard, to report to Fifth Air Force.

The correspondent, who had strolled over behind Pell, had heard it all. He brought it up as he resumed his interview: "Did you know him, Lieutenant?"

"Cleve Connell?"

"Is that who it was?"

Pell nodded, listening to the hurried sound of the pencil. He knew its magic. He paused at length. He had a thoughtful expression on his face. His eyes, those exceptional eyes, had apparently seen things he could not tell about, and that he never could be old enough not to be too young to have seen.

"He was a george guy," Pell said.

"George?"

"That's right. The best, the greatest. He taught me everything I know about this business. It was just that he didn't get the breaks himself."

"You were pretty close to him?"

"He was my flight leader," Pell said, "but he was like a brother. I just don't know what to say, I can't believe they got him."

The correspondent lived on his judgment, too, and he was no fool. He watched Pell closely. He could not subdue a sense of suspicion, but then he became a little ashamed of himself. They were fighting here, up in the hostile skies of North Korea. There was no fraud in that. Pell seemed a little—was it aware? but every word rang poignantly true.

"Don't write any of that, though," Pell said unexpectedly.

"These are just my notes."

"I know, but people don't understand what it's like. It wouldn't mean anything."

"That depends on how well I handle it."

"Well, I hope you're a good handler," Pell said. He smiled wanly. His candor was disarming.

The article was carried in a national magazine. It was a great success. There was a photograph of Pell in the cockpit, stark and memorable. A whole country found its heroism in his face.

For Cleve, the war had ended in those final minutes of solitude he had always dreaded. He was carried as "missing in action." If there had been a last cry, electrically distilled through air, it had gone unheard as he fell to the multitudes he feared. They had overcome him in the end, tenaciously, scissoring past him, taking him down. Their heavy shots had splashed into him, and they had followed all the way, firing as they did, with that contagious passion peculiar to hunters.

ALSO BY JAMES SALTER

BURNING THE DAYS

In the course of seven decades, James Salter has experienced enough romance for any dozen lives, piloting jet fighters at speeds approaching that of sound, hammering out screenplays with Robert Redford, and falling in love with one of John Huston's mistresses. In this stunningly eloquent memoir, he commemorates it all with a precision of thought and language that is at once clarifying and intoxicating.

Memoir/0-394-75948-6

LIGHT YEARS

This exquisite, resonant novel is a brilliant portrait of marriage by a contemporary American master. It is the story of Nedra and Viri, whose life is centered around ingenious games with their children, enviable friends, and near-perfect days passed skating on a frozen river or sunning on the beach. But even as he lingers over the surface of their marriage, James Salter lets us see the fine cracks that are spreading through it, flaws that will eventually mar the lovely picture beyond repair.

Fiction/Literature/0-679-74073-2